Night and the Texas Sky

A fucking novel

By Travis Baker

For Scott and Seamus,

For those who lived and those that died.

Cloud Walking

When you walk on clouds be careful.

When you walk on clouds, beware,

And never look beneath your feet

To see what's under there.

-Shel Silverstein

Prologue

Twenty one years ago an Army nurse discovers Vietnamese poetry and returns to Houston unknowingly carrying the gestating manifestation of cross-pollinating a hoa lan orchid with an Irish rose. She will name him Sean, after her grandfather.

Twenty years seven months ago a father calls his new daughter "Kitten" for the first time.

Twenty years ago a woman traces the scar on her belly with her finger as she watches a nurse feed her perfect little wonder with a bottle. She has not decided on a name yet. She thinks it will be Karen or possibly Isabelle.

Nineteen years and five months ago a 10 lbs. 5 oz. baby boy is crapped out after 23 hours of labor. He is named Zachary partly because the mother swears it will be her last.

Day

1.

He stood before her with a blade in his hand.

He stood before her naked and smelling of Texas heat. Even with the sun just climbing, the walls of the apartment dripped with sweat and the stink of rot rose from the musty carpet. He felt the place slowly folding over him, like wet cardboard collapsing.

Zac watched as the hand holding the blade moved forward; watched its razor edge trace the curve of her breast, the breast that had been painted in pinks, purple and blues. He drew the knife point in ripples across the canvas. The thick air vibrated with the hum of locusts.

He had already made a slow circuit of the front room of his first floor shotgun apartment, slashing and slicing the Exacto across every failed attempt to capture life in the scrawlings of a pencil scratch. Half sheets of newsprint floated down like memories of falling snow while the charcoals on heavy illustration board dropped with impact. He'd gone after the posters next, cutting Johnny Rotten to the core, dismembering Sting, dividing Bauhaus neatly in two. They weren't his posters. They were his

7

dead brother's and his dead brother was dead and all he had left of him were posters, records, D&D books, crumpled attempts at drawing a portrait and three paintings. Of the three paintings, the man over the bricked up fireplace, the child over the sofa and the woman in the bedroom, only she remained, as yet, undamaged.

The man was a self-portrait James had done when he was eighteen and just started at the Houston Institute of Art, just before he'd dropped out. It was James at his best, in his best vintage vest with his high purple Mohawk, his ripped up jeans and his Doc Martins. His face was wide. He smiled. His dark eyes followed Zac around the room.

Zac took the painting down and stabbed him in the head. He stabbed again in the chest and watched as an imagined geyser of blood shot forth, drenching, drowning him. He stabbed again, and then again and then over and over so that, now, the man was lost and only tattered rags hung limp in the morning haze.

He climbed the sofa to attack the child. It was a picture of his own self from when he was five and trying to draw a truck at the table. James must have been thirteen at the time but he didn't paint it until he was twenty. He'd given it to their mother for Christmas that year. Zac took it with him when he moved out and now cut out its head and then its arms and then its legs. They fell with flops behind the couch. Zac stepped down, leaving an

8

empty frame upon the wall as if something vile had carried the kid off to feed hungry devils.

He went to the bedroom.

Her face was turned away. She couldn't look.

She was his dead brother's dead girlfriend. She was naked, her pink painted breasts fluffy and full. The folds of her belly twisted towards her hips and the length of her thigh invited the viewer to slide into her from behind. It was almost exactly as Zac found her in that tangle of bodies two years ago. She would have been soft and enveloping. It must have been like pushing into a pillow. Zac had dreamed many times of her, explored the limits of flesh and friction many times thinking of the softness of her, her last gasp, a gunshot, her muted cry.

Zac got hard. He regarded his penis, his big stupid thing, engorged and purple headed and then the blade, razor thin, silver, and small, and her behind her curtain of acrylic paint. The canvas wore a rubber, protection from his penis but not the blade. He put it to her neck. He held it there and wrapped his hand around the shaft of himself and began to push and pull and twist, thinking about that breast and how it was made of dried rubber and dried rubbers on hot Houston asphalt and pushing into pillows.

His heart pumped hard and his breath came quick. His teeth clamped. He felt the come welling up in his balls. He came with a looping spurt. Some of it slapped against the wall, while some fell to the carpet and two drops landed on his toes. He slashed the blade across her throat and saw the blood spurting out into a blood and cum stained everything.

He felt empty. He felt sick and sweat covered. He felt fevered and reached out his hand to the wall to steady himself. He saw her bleeding, bleeding out and down, down the wall, into the carpet but when he looked down he saw no blood squishing up between his toes just slops of milky seed.

He heard the phone ring and ring. It had been ringing off and on and on and off for three days.

He staggered back from the wall and went to the front room. He looked up at the molded molding framing the ceiling and for the thousandth time thought the coffee colored stain in the far corner looked like a monkey.

He picked up the phone.

"What?" He looked out the window to the side yard and the weathered washed out fence beyond.

"Zac?"

"Yeah?"

"It's Sean!"

"Who?"

"We met at that party at Amy's house the other month. We talked about you joining my band."

Zac's attention moved between the slats of the fence and out into the yard beyond and the space and sky beyond that. He had not slept well. The phone kept ringing He was thinking that the world didn't end, it just stretched out infinitely, beyond the blue brown sky, beyond the thinning air and into space where comets collide and out past space, out beyond the void, out beyond infinity. Zac shook his head. The greasy, sweaty strands of long, dyed-blue black hairs already starting to fall out of the top of his head tickled across the skin shaved sides.

"There is no heaven. Only the void. The voids. The space between the slats is a void," he said.

"I hear you, man," Sean said. "Dude, hang on a second..." Zac heard Sean put down the phone. He looked around for his smokes. He heard Sean say to someone, "Kitten, come here! Listen to this!"

He heard a girl's voice, what sounded like a little girl's voice, say, "What?" He saw the smokes on the little table his sister had left behind when she moved out and let him have the place. Zac put the blade down and picked up his smokes. He slid a cigarette out of the pack and hunted around for his brother's old Zippo.

The little girl's voice, sounding like strawberry-flavored bubble-gum, said, "What's up?"

He saw the squat silver lighter on top of one of his brother's old Black Flag albums which sat on top of a stack of his brother's other old

11

albums. His brother had always kept his albums in plastic protectors so the covers wouldn't get damaged. His brother used to slide the vinyls out ever so carefully, holding them with a thumb on the edge and a finger in the middle, careful not to touch the grooves. He used to spray them with a delicate cleaner and wipe them with a special cloth. He changed the needle on his record player regularly. Zac didn't own a record player. He never took the albums out. He flipped through them now and again and again and could hear the Sex Pistols, Joy Division, Led Zeppelin, the Dead Kennedy's and the Cars playing in his brother's old room. He could see his brother bent over his guitar, trying to learn the melodies. He could feel the heavy bass strings under his fingers because he wanted to help his brother out. He could smell the cleaning spray

"The world is covered in rubber, blood and cum," Zac said. "And..." He picked up the lighter, snapped it open and lit his smoke. "... There's nothing to wipe it up with."

There was a pause, a breath and the ever so slightly wet sound of two lips parting. Then Zac heard the tickle of metal against teeth and the voice, still sounding like bubble-gum but the green apple flavor crystal kind, said, "And underneath is cracking concrete, crumbled butter-cream cake and lies."

Zac blew out a brown blue fume. He went back to the bedroom, dragging the phone along behind him like a little dog without any legs,

12

bumping and spanking along the sidewalk. He regarded the painting of Tori and the wound across her neck. He cradled the phone in his neck and reached his hand out, slipping his fingers through the slice.

"I just cut her throat," Zac said.

"Whose throat?" Kitten asked.

"My dead brother's dead girlfriend's."

"Is she there with you?"

"No," Zac lowered his head. He looked down at his feet. "Sort of. She's a painting." His finger curled into the cut.

"Disappointing," Kitten said. "Here's Sean."

Zac ripped the canvas down in a long, slow tear.

"Zac!" Sean said.

"I was just going to slash my wrists," Zac said.

"I was going to throw myself off the Transco Tower last week," Sean said. "I took the elevator to the top. There's a service door. It says EMERGENCY EXIT and this was a fucking emergency in need of an exit." Sean snorted and tittered. "I was going to go up there and jump off. Take one last flying leap, you know. But then I remembered this kid, Charlie, tossed himself off the Shell building last year and landed on a jogger. Anyway, about the band, we need a bassist."

Zac took a long drag from the smoke. There was a pile of clothes next to his brother's old illustration desk. On the desk was an ashtray, two

13

empty diet Coke cans, an empty tape dispenser, a jammed stapler, a tackle box filled with colored pencils, thises, thats and other things. Under the pile of shorts, shirts, socks and underwear was his old black bass leaning against a dusty amp. Since moving up to this, his sister's old apartment almost over a year ago, Zac had played the thing twice. Both times he'd played the same long slow underbelly to a song called "Bleed to Nothing." It was the song they would play when they rehearsed. James and Kurt would pass a bong around, fill the air with tie-dyed smoke and disintegrate. The song had no beginning and no end. It came and went and faded away.

"I haven't really done that in a while."

"It's not a problem. Raven will get you up to speed."

"Who's Raven?"

"She's the guitarist."

"Maybe I could be a guitarist."

Zac had always wanted to be a guitarist. His mother had insisted that her children learn an instrument and she'd taught all three of them the piano from when they were very young. In school, James tried out the violin but eventually moved onto guitar because that's where the chicks were. Lori learned the cello, the flute and the clarinet so she could be in the marching band. Zac was given a stand-up bass in middle school because he was the biggest kid in the class and his fingers didn't fit on much else.

"Not necessary, thank you." Sean said.

"Okay." Zac went over to the pile and dusted the clothes off with his hand. James had given it to him for his thirteenth birthday and said if he learned how to play better than Sid Vicious he could be in his band, The Snakes. It really didn't take that long.

"What's Kitten doing?"

"Singing."

"Lot of animals involved."

"You don't even know."

"What are you doing?"

"Drums," Sean said. "I told you that at the party."

"I don't really remember the party." Smoke got in Zac's eyes and he had to rub it out with the back of his wrist. "I don't really remember you, actually."

"I'm the half-Vietnamese/half-Irish kid. Dark skin, blue eyes."

"Oh, right."

Zac remembered they'd met by the keg. This little guy bouncing up and down passing around a joint. He wore red low top Chucks and he'd written FUCK and YOU on the toes so that if you stood in front of him you could read it plainly. His band had just broken up because the bassist had joined the Marines and the singer had OD'd and gone into rehab. Zac had remembered he'd mentioned he'd played the bass. He'd forgotten how he'd

15

gotten to the party but he remembered how he got home, stumbling and stuttering.

"So anyway we need a bassist because we're playing a party tonight and I've been trying to call you for three days now."

Some wires are thinner than others. Some wires are drawn too tight for too long and must eventually snap. The wire whips back and out, slashing the air and everything in its path. Minutes ago he had been that wire, slicing the canvases and the thick hanging air. He'd forgotten about his skin and the costumes worn upon it. He'd only felt the flight. Now he went limp, hanging in dissembled form, just lying on the ground in a puddle.

"I need a shower," he said.

"So take a shower. We'll pick you up and get over to Steele's warehouse!"

"Steele?"

"The pro-wrestler. You heard of him?"

"Yeah. My dad took me to a show once." Zac filled his lungs with smoke.

"Dude's got a wrestling ring in the warehouse. We can jump off the top rope!"

"Beats jumping off a building," Zac said to Sean.

"Seriously, dude."

"I don't know." He wasn't just in the puddle, he was the puddle. He was the murky dregs collected in a dent in the pavement waiting to slowly evaporate as mosquitoes lay eggs and an oily sheen slops rainbows on the curb.

"You doing anything better today?" Sean said.

"Not really."

"Sweet!"

Zac tapped on the cigarette and ash floated off from the tip. It dropped in gentle arcs to the carpet and settled on the frayed hairs. "What's our name?"

There was a pause and a silence. "Well, see this is why I've been calling you," Sean said and then he went on about how they had gotten to talking at Amy's party and gotten to talking about how Zac had a dead brother and sort of how that happened and the band was going to be sort of a gothic punky grungy thing and what a cool name for a band Double Murder Suicide would be.

The phone grew hot. The damp room was charged static. The folding walls turned to stone and iron. Zac heard the sizzle of a cigarette between Sean's lips and then the slow, swirling exhale. It all echoed inside Zac and then fell down a deep dark pit. He listened for it to hit and heard the crash down in the depths. He waited for the drums to beat and the monsters to swarm up from the dark. Zac closed his eyes and sat down on his bed.

"What's going on," he heard the bubblegum voice say from afar.

"Silence," Sean said.

"Gimme," and the phone was handed off.

Zac was all dried up. He'd evaporated. He was a dull mud colored stain smeared across a dull gray crack.

"Zac?" she said in strawberry.

"Yeah?"

"Where are you?"

"I don't know," he said. He didn't. He looked around the room. "I'm in my sister's old apartment surrounded by my brother's old stuff. Nothing here is mine."

The voice on the phone asked him if he had a cigarette lit and when he said he did it told him to touch the tip to the inside of his arm. "I'll do it with you," she said.

The cigarette held between his fingers was nearly spent but a little red cherry was still burning bright. He wedged the phone between his shoulder and cheek. He placed the cigarette to his left wrist. He felt nothing and then he did.

"Hold it there," she said to him.

The smoke that screwed away from his skin blossomed orange and green.

"Can you feel, how you feel, that feeling of feeling again?"

"Yes," he said. His teeth began to grind, his lips began to peel. Cradled in the crook of his neck he heard her breath drawing in.

"Crush it into you," she hissed.

He pressed the cigarette hard into his flesh and fire infected the blood that pumped inside his veins. His fingers curled into a fist and then released then curled in again. He shuddered and a tear ran from his eye.

"Stop," she said.

He pulled the spent and broken cigarette away. Smudges of ash and tobacco flakes had melted into an angry red bubble and squeal.

Her voice wasn't bubble gum any more. It was a sickly syrup. "The pain is pain. It hurts. You can see the hurt and feel the hurt. It isn't a deep hollow inside yourself. It isn't rattling around in your chest."

"Thank you," he said.

"You're welcome."

"I need to take a shower," Zac said.

"Wish I could join you," came a watermelon lollipop flavored whisper and then a harsh click.

Zac put the phone back in its cradle and set it down on the bed. He stood, went over and dropped the cigarette in the ashtray on the desk. He held up his arm. The ash smudges almost made a face. He raised his arms, stretching, putting his hands flat on the ceiling, pushing at it, feeling the painted boards bend and the beams rise ever so slightly much.

The phone rang again. He dropped his arms, bent over and picked it up.

"Yeah?"

"Dude, it's Sean again. Where do you live?"

Zac told him. Sean said they'd pick him up in half an hour, said it was going to fucking rock, then hung up.

Zac put the phone back. He stood. He looked around. His vision drifted softly over the fallen rags, the shreds, rips and tears that covered the floor and furniture. He hefted the bass up from its dank corner, holding it by the neck at arm's length.

2.

"He sounded sad," Kitten said, sliding her black satin gloves over her tartan skirt and black tights.

"He sounded dead," Sean said from the cavernous red leather back seat of Raven's '58 Buick Roadmaster. "He found his brother and his brother's girlfriend and…" Kitten's hair was a lot like the car, black with red accents. She wore wide black shades that flared out at the wings. She turned to look at Sean as he took a bite of the breakfast taco he'd gotten from Dos Amigos, "…his brother's best friend…hold on." Sean had to stop talking for a second because the egg and pork juices were running down his hand and he didn't want them to get on his favorite lime green t-shirt or his red plaid pants.

"You're not dripping shit on my car are you?" Raven said.

"No!" But the juice was running down Sean's arm. He didn't have much room to maneuver because even if the back seat was about the size of the Astrodome, there was a guitar case wedged against an amp that was sitting on a PA next to him. The paper bag was on the floor between his feet. Doing a delicate dance of gravitational gymnastics, he managed to guide the dripping taco juice into the bag and extract two napkins at the same time.

"I told you not to eat in the car!" She craned her neck up, trying to watch Sean in the mirror and the road at the same time. "And don't get any shit on my guitar case."

"It's fine," Sean said, mashing the last half of the taco into his mouth. "No drips or drops anywhere."

"I'm fucking serious, Sean."

"I know you are, baby." Sean wiped at the corner of his mouth with the side of his palm.

"So what happened?" Kitten said. Her elbow hung out the window bouncing the brilliant light of the day off of bare pink pale skin.

Sean wiped his face again. "He found his brother and his brother's girlfriend and his brother's best friend all in bed together."

"So?"

Raven made the turn from West Dallas onto Waugh, the great boat of a car tilting to port and the white-wall tires bouncing and rolling.

"So," Sean said, digging around in his hip pouch for the little wooden case that held the half-a-joint he had pinched out when they stopped for breakfast. He had to push the plastic-wrapped sheets of acid to the side and the 8-ball of coke he'd promised to Steele back down. The case was wedged in the corner by the bottle of X and his Big Mama lighter. "They were all dead." He pulled out the case, slid back the siding, pulled out the joint then put the case back and pulled out the Big Mama lighter which, when he struck it, sent up a six-inch flame. "That's what he said at the party, anyway. Kind of a depressing conversation, actually."

"Do not burn my car!" Raven squawked, eyeing him in the rear view.

"Relax," Sean said. He tossed his long, sleek pony-tail to one side, leaned his head to the other and lit up. The paper crackled and the weed smoldered. He let the flame die and breathed deeply in. This would settle him, this would keep him right. He just needed the calm that came with smoke. He needed it to settle on him and drift. He needed a soft white cloud because underneath his skin he could feel sharp rocks.

Raven's eyes returned to the street as they came to the intersection with Milo. A beat-up pick-up truck grumbled past them and then a sleek SUV. She watched and waited for a proper opening. The Buick needed a lot of space. When there was enough of a cushion to taxi the space shuttle down the street, she pulled out and turned right.

Kitten watched for the mockingbirds that would swoop down into the street and swipe a crushed French fry or abandoned eggroll and then fly back to their perches after avoiding by inches a feather blasting blow from a Camaro.

23

Sean held the smoke as long as he could and then blew it out in a rush. "They were all naked," he choked out.

Kitten turned her head and looked at Sean.

"Naked?"

Sean gulped down another hit. "Yup."

She turned back and watched the blistered world slide by.

"Yup," came another gulp from the back. "Some seriously fucked up shit. I've been through some seriously fucked up shit but that kid has some seriously, seriously fucked up shit." Sean felt the light green haze descend upon him like a cloud pulled down from the sky by butterflies. He was warm and happy, snuggled up in a red leather cocoon.

Kitten clicked the little silver barbell through her tongue against the little silver hoops at the corners of her mouth. She knew about naked men and gunshot wounds. She smelled again her father's sickly sweet breath, felt for a fleeting moment the crushing weight and heard the graveled voice whispering, "Kitten...my sweet Kitten." She touched a satin covered finger to her lips. He had given his little Kitten her first pair of satin gloves. They were red. They covered up the bruises and then they covered up the burns.

"Some fucked up shit," Sean said.

They came to the edge of Montrose, where they bumped up against the invisible line where being a white kid with white skin, bleached out white hair and thick black eye-liner drawn down in Egyptian-style circles

24

and driving a cherry sweet ride was no longer the height of fashion but just asking for trouble. Raven smiled. She wanted trouble. Or at least she thought she did, she thought. She held the steering wheel with her left hand and dropped her right under the seat to caress the metal butt of her Glock 9mm in its leather holster. The magazine held 18 rounds and she had loaded it in an alternating armor piercing and black talon fashion like her father had taught her. That way, if the asshole was wearing armor, he'd still get a clean smooth hole through and through and if he wasn't then the black talon would blossom inside his chest and serrate every major organ in his body. She liked guns. She liked guitars. She had to admit to herself that her most intimate relationships were with inanimate objects. She smiled but then she slid her tongue across her teeth. They were ragged from all the bile she passed back up between them and she moved her hand back to the wheel.

Sean looked down at the side of the door, at the red leather lining because he remembered the last night he'd been home and he didn't want to. It was nothing. It wasn't even worth a moment but the moment wouldn't leave him. His right leg started tapping up and down. He laughed a stuttering girlish giggle of a laugh, pinched out the last of the roach and tossed it out the window as Raven squeezed the Buick down a small side street.

"Is this right?" she said.

"There he is!" Sean leaned forward and pointed at the young man in a sleeveless black t-shirt, deep set eyes, fading blue hair flopping over in an uninspired Mohawk, sitting on the front steps of a peeling and sinking row house next to a long, black electric bass and a worn amp.

Raven let the car drift to a stop and leaned towards Kitten to get a look at him as he stood up. "Jesus, how fucking tall is he?"

"Really fucking tall," Sean said and opened his door.

"Well, he looks like a bassist," Raven said.

Kitten pulled her lower lip in with her teeth as Zac stood, hoisted the amp in one hand and dragged the bass by the other and walked slowly towards the car. He walked with his shoulders hunched, in a laconic stride.

"Yo," Sean said, coming around the back, smiling, laughing, raising his right hand for a mid-five. Zac set the amp down and complied. He remembered the energy that popped off of Sean like fireflies released from a jar. He remembered the long soft hair and the eyes the color of tropical oceans. He remembered the white t-shirt but not the lime green pants but he remembered the shoes.

"Looks like a squirrel saying hello to a bear," Kitten said.

Raven cackled.

Zac looked over at her and she stopped. The girl that had laughed had white hair and a long sharp face behind 60's style sunglasses. The other girl had rich red lips, like strawberries. He pushed a flopping stray hair behind his ear.

"I think we can squeeze the amp in the front," Sean gestured to the car, "and you and your bass in the back."

"I have a car," Zac said.

"No, no, no," Sean waved his arm, "we can all fit. Kitten can sit on my lap."

"Why do I have to sit on your lap?"

"So we can all fit," Sean said.

Kitten hung herself a little bit further out the window.

"Why can't I sit on his lap?" she said.

A small bright flutter of light raced around Zac's eyeballs.

"Because you won't fit," Sean said and took a step towards the car.

"I don't know," Kitten said as she lowered her shades and smoldered her gilded green eyes in a wondrously melodramatic way that she was only half consciously aware of. "We might fit just fine, sugar."

Sean shook his head. "Just get out for a second," he said.

Kitten shoved her shades back into place and heaved the door open. As she stepped out Zac registered the subtle turns of Kitten's belly revealed by the naughty little punker chick clothing. She was tiny. A kitten not just in name but in stature. He noted the silver hoop through the belly button. The two hoops and one stud in her nose. The dozens of little studs and

27

hoops in her ears. The little hoops at the corners of her mouth. She wore herself like it was Halloween.

"You must have a hard time with metal detectors," he said to her.

"I avoid them as much as possible," she said back.

Sean picked up Zac's amp and shoved it in the front seat as Kitten tapped the little metal ball in her tongue against the back of her teeth. She took three steps towards him. The immensity of him blocked out the sight of the house beyond and nearly everything else except a small corner of sky. She circled him, gaining slightly higher ground towards the house. His arms were like slabs of meat He smelled of Old Spice and something else.

"Let me see," she said.

Zac switched the bass to his other hand and held out his blistered arm. She took it in satin gloves and traced a little circle with her finger. She sighed and said she would kiss it and make it better.

She held his arm and lowered her cherry tinted lips. On the wiry hairs along his forearm he felt her breath and on his skin the delicate press of tender velvet.

Raven looked up from her exertions with Sean, trying to slide the amp in without ripping or scratching the red leather seats. She could only see the back of him and only the legs of her, between his. She saw him lift his chin and shudder his spine. "What, is she sucking his dick?"

Sean turned and looked just as Zac's head snapped forward with a primal howl.

"Hope not," he said.

Soft lips had been rent by vicious teeth. Pain on pain struck through him. He dropped the bass and was about to press his hand to her face when she let go. With a giggle and a hop she danced back to the car.

Sean got out and stood next to the door.

"She bite you?" he said.

"Yeah," Zac said. He looked down at his arm. Deep impressions cut white against flushed skin. From two of those seeped beads of blood.

"She does that." Sean smiled. "Come on, let's bowl."

Sean dropped himself into the car and waited for Kitten to pounce on top of him which she did right after she wiped at her mouth with her black gloved hand.

Zac felt the muscles in his jaw flex and ripple. He looked down the street at the cars parked all along and the oak trees hanging low in front of cracking houses. He heard the cackling of starlings swarming in the branches, rattling the leaves. He stooped to pick the bass. He would have gone back inside and locked the door but his amp was already in the car so what choice did he have? He went around the back to the other side of the car where a thin, white face framed by long, white hair offset by black painted lips stared out at him.

29

"Hey," he said.

"Hi," Raven said back.

"Cool car."

"You're a lefty," she said. "I noticed the strings."

Zac looked at his strings. They were upside down. He wondered why he was looking at his strings. He knew they were upside down. He stopped looking at his strings and looked at the girl who had made him do such a silly thing. Her skin seemed to be drawn too tight at the bones yet too loose in the hollows. "Yep," he said and opened the door. He bent forward and slid the bass next to the guitar case that was next to the amp that was stacked on top of the PA. He folded himself in and the Buick sagged with his weight.

Sean turned his head as best he could. It was like a cartoon the way Zac was stuffed in back there. "Comfy?" he said.

Zac nodded as Raven let off the brake and rolled the Buick out.

Sean smiled and turned his head back to the front. He adjusted his hips under Kitten, draped one arm over the rippled surface of Zac's amp and the other along Kitten's leg. They were all crammed in there, them and all their stuff, because he had gotten them there. He'd found them in forgotten corners, dusted them off to put them on display. This was happening. This was his. He started to hum a familiar tune as Raven drove them away.

3.

In fourth grade a girl named Ruby had come up to Zac after school and told him he was now her boyfriend. "Okay," he'd said. She smiled and nodded and went back to tell her friends. The next day she invited him over to her house but he couldn't go because he had football practice but the day after that he went over and her mother made them hot chocolate in the microwave and they spent some time in her room listening to Thriller. They tried kissing. Ruby had to get up on her knees to reach Zac's mouth. Their hands remained pressed firmly to their sides as their lips met and Ruby tried to slip her delicate little tongue between Zac's clenched teeth. The next day Zac got a note from Ruby's best friend in the lunch line telling him that Ruby was breaking up with him and that he needed to work on his kissing.

As the Buick glided down West Gray, past the shacks of the 5th Ward that crowded around gravel streets before slipping under I-45 into the deserted streets of downtown, Zac very much felt as if he had just been told he was someone's boyfriend and he would need to work on his kissing.

Sean was bouncing Kitten up and down in his seat and doing something a lot like singing. "I will not eat them on a boat/I will not eat them with a goat/I will not eat them here nor there/I will not eat them ANYWHERE! Green eggs and ham! Green eggs and ham! Green eggs and ham! Sam I am! Green eggs and ham! Green eggs and ham! Green eggs and ham! I am Saaaaaaaaaaammmmm!" He concluded with a rollicking drum roll across the dash.

Raven slashed her arm at his hands. "Watch the fucking car!"

"Ease up!" Sean retraced his hands around Kitten's waist.

"I'm not singing that," Kitten said.

Sean gave Kitten's a squeeze. "You don't have to sing that one, Kitten. Zac and I can sing that one."

Kitten twisted half herself around. "Then what am I supposed to do?" she said.

"Play the tambourine." He leaned forward again and draped himself over the front seat as they left downtown, crossed under I-59 and drifted into the warehouse district. "Take this left."

"Why doesn't Raven sing?" Kitten said.

Raven snorted as she slowed the car, directed it to the left and rumbled it over some train tracks.

Sean shook his head.

"What?" Kitten said.

"You really don't want to hear me sing," Raven said.

"It's not pleasant," Sean added.

32

Kitten lowered her sunglasses. "I hear you humming all the time at the record store."

"Guitar melodies." Raven scoped her surroundings. The relics and remains of buildings that once stored cotton, sugar, rice and watermelons to be sent off onto ships around the world hunkered here and there, interspaced with weed crowded lots and rusting fences falling down. "Ravens are not known for their beauteous songs."

Sean waved at a bug that had flown in. "She sounds like a drowning cat."

"Fuck you," Raven said. "Where the hell are we going?"

"Just up the street," Sean said. "And then over a few blocks. You'll see it. There's big giant spider over the gate."

"A real spider?" Kitten tried to shift herself off Sean's lap.

"Yes," Sean laughed. "A giant ten foot real spider."

"Fuck you. I don't like spiders and that better not be your little penis poking into me."

"Thing's got a mind of its own. Turn here."

Zac could hear the tires squelch as Raven took a left. The car slid under the shadow of a shell of a building and emerged onto a trash-strewn, pot-holed lane bordered by an abandoned lot covered in scrub brush that was infested with old tires and worn out mattresses. At the next street a sparkling chain-link fence began and ran all the way around the block on the left.

"We're here," Sean said. "Check it out." Zac leaned his head to get a view. Woven into the fencing were metal dragons and chrome snakes. Halfway up the block a giant spider tortured out of rusted rebar clung to a wide gate.

"Kick ass," Raven said as she pulled the Buick up under the spider.

Sean opened his door and helped Kitten slide off him. He stood, adjusted his pants slightly and skipped over to a call box that had been framed by a fanged metal skull that shined menacingly hot under the blasting sun. Kitten turned in small circles as he pushed a little white button.

Zac got out as well and stretched his arms wide. Sweat dripped from his pits. It ran in rivulets down his arms and biceps. He wiped his hands on his shorts and dug out his smokes. Kitten looked up at him.

Sean pressed the button again.

"Is anyone home?" Raven said, sticking her head out the window.

Sean bounced on his toes. He could see a truck parked by the building. "He's here," he said, and pressed the button again.

Zac turned away from Kitten and stared off towards the sparkling spires built from black gold that comprised downtown Houston. Kitten crunched a rock under her boot as Raven drummed her fingers on the steering wheel. The heat rose from the hood of the car like bar codes. She could see notes on it, long riffs and short bursts rising up into the air. She wanted to be setting up her amps and effects board. She wanted to be tuning up. She wanted to be lost in the sonic elsewhere. She didn't want to be sitting here sweating her tits off, of which, she knew, she had precious little. Her mom used to stuff her bras with paper and pads for the pageants she'd been dragged to since she was three. Even when she put on weight, nothing happened, so now she never wore the stupid things and let the hair grow under her arms, wore baggy clothes and didn't give a shit about anything except ripping apart oxygen molecules with her guitar.

"Yeah?" came a voice from the box.

"Steele!" shouted Sean.

"Yeah?" came the voice.

"It's Sean!"

"Who?"

Kitten pinched at her arms. Raven dug her fingernails into the wheel.

"Sean!" Sean said. "I brought my new band. We're playing a party here tonight!"

"We are?" squizzled the voice.

Sean kicked at a rock near the post that the box was attached to.

"Yeah, man. We talked about this at your art show!"

"Oh, right," said the voice. "See you tonight!"

"Steele!"

"What?"

"We have to set up and practice!"

"Oh."

"Yeah."

"Okay."

Sean leaned towards the box. "I got that stuff you wanted," he said quietly.

"Now I remember," crackled the voice.

"Of course you do," Sean mumbled, glancing over at Kitten, Raven and Zac.

"What?" said the box.

"Nothing! Open the gate, please!"

The great spider overhead began to shake and tremble and for a moment Raven worried that it would suddenly pounce on her precious baby but with a grind of gears the gate slid wide and beyond was revealed an open gravel yard and a large, corrugated metal warehouse.

Sean waved her in. "Park near the bay doors."

Kitten hopped in and Raven pulled the car inside the fence and wove around piles of salvaged metal strewn about to the open doors. Two black dogs came lolling and huffing out of the bay and then a man holding a metal cup, wearing tighty-whities and pink flip-flops stepped from the

36

shadows of the building and pointed to a spot next to a neon blue king cab pick-up with the name STEELE airbrushed along the side. Raven wheeled the car around, backed it up and parked. She turned off the ignition, pulled out the key on its Mexican cross key chain, opened the door and stepped out onto something brown and squishy. She looked down.

"What the fuck!" she said.

"Shit, sorry about that," said the man in his underwear. "Yard's full of little grenades."

Raven looked up at the man strolling towards her, taking a sip from his cup and scratching his tighty-whitied ass. He was not a very tall man, shorter than her, but his muscles bulged like an inflatable raft, stretching shaved and tanned skin at improbably veined angles.

"Bitches, you know." He shrugged and took another drink. "I'm Steele." He held out a thick hand. She took it and they shook. He handled her gently, but there was something lingering about it, a creeping sense of possession as he held her hand a second too long.

"Raven," she said and tugged her hand away.

"I like it," he said. His engorged pecs popped up and down.

Steele sipped from his cup and turned away as Sean approached. Raven ground her boot across the gravel. "Be careful where you step, Kitten," she said and looked around for a twig or something. Kitten opened her door, eyed the ground suspiciously and then hissed as one of the dogs came slobbering at her, sniffing and lolling out its tongue.

"Hairball!" Steele yelled and the dog gave Kitten a sad shrug of its ears and turned away. Steele turned back to Sean. "What's up you half-gook Irish bastard!"

"My man, Steele!" Sean shouted and thrust out his hand which Steele slapped, gripped and then released.

Raven located a stick, took it up in her spindly fingers and sat back onto her seat, perching her boot by the heel, trying to keep it away from the other boot or her car door while digging out the sludgy poop from the combat treads.

The dogs wagged and leapt towards Zac as he came up.

"Hairball! Dumbass! Down!" Steele yelled but the dogs ignored him.

"That's all right," said Zac. He gave them his hands to sniff, rubbed their heads, scratched their butts and soon both of them were belly up, legs twitching in the air as he gave them a good belly rub.

"You got a way with the ladies," Steele said to him. Zac looked up.

"I saw you wrestle the Big Kahuna a few years ago," he said.

Steele snapped his head back and laughed. "That fucking guy," he said and took a sip from the cup. Zac watched him turn and look over at the girls. Raven was bending forward, working a stick in her boot and didn't catch him taking a long look down the three-sizes-too-large-long-sleeve black t-shirt she wore over a two-times-too-large black t-shirt with no sleeves. Nor did she see his lips move into a disappointed sigh.

Kitten saw the look though, as she came warily around the car. She saw the look, the sigh, and then his greasy grin when he looked up at her, adjusted himself and then held out his hand.

"Hi there," he said.

Kitten glowered at the hand. "Maybe if you hadn't just played with your balls," she said.

"Feisty," Steele said, dropping his hand. "I like it!"

He was too close now. She could smell his tanning solution and see the fine white lines that latticed his forehead. Two of them were fresh and scabbed red. Steele raised his hand and touched them gently.

"Folks like a little blood," he said. "Trick of the trade. Keep a little bit of razor in your lip then when it's time, go down, give a little slice, come back up…" Steele rose, slid his hand over his face and growled. "The crimson mask!" He laughed. His whole body shook and then he seized into snorts. "Folks love that shit," he said.

"Where should we set up?" Sean asked.

Steele wiped his eyes and regained his breath. "This way," and he waved them all into the warehouse.

39

In the cavernous expanse to their right was a pro-wrestling ring. Rubber coated ropes stretched to create a five-foot high fence around a square platform that was four feet off the ground.

"That's the ring of course," Steele said. "Y'all can try it out if you want. Gets pretty crazy in there at parties." Steele spit on the floor. "Around it are my sculpture stations." He popped a bicep that seemed to pile up on itself like a melting ice cream sundae. Around the ring were a bench press, squat station, lat bar, dumbbell rack and various other machines of physical improvement. Steele turned to the left. "Over there are my other sculpture stations," and indicated with a nod of his head the metal tables, welding tools, electric and propane chargers, wrenches, pipes, pipe-benders and saws that filled a considerable space beyond which were three, fifteen-foot-tall aisles stacked with an eclectic assortment of scrap metal.

"Where do you get all your metal?" Raven said before she could stop herself and wished she had stopped herself because he immediately made a crack about where she could find the hardest piece of metal within fifty miles which was funny only to him.

"I find most of my material right around in the lots." He waved a hand towards the outside world where Hairball could be seen sniffing at Dumbass's butt until Dumbass nipped at her. Steele took a drink from his cup. Zac kept looking over at the ring.

"Want to give it whirl, big guy?"

40

Zac squinted. "My brother said it was all bullshit."

Steele laughed. "You tell your brother to take a shot to the back of the head with a steel chair and tell me its bullshit!" He looked over at Sean and laughed some more.

"He's dead," Zac said.

Steele stopped laughing. His eyes tightened up as his pecs popped three times. Kitten shifted in her boots. "You do that a lot?" Steele said.

"What?" Zac said.

Steele spit on the floor again. "Set people up like that," he said.

Zac's eyes zigzagged from Steele's face down to his flip-flopped feet. There was always a way to slip his dead brother into everyday conversation. There was always a way to make people stop and think about the dead, his dead, the thing he dragged along in the dust behind him. Steele stepped close to him, his pale eyes squinting out of fleshy folds.

"I could drop you on the ground and have you screaming for mama in three seconds, kid. You just remember that."

Zac felt the sudden clutch at his throat, the heave of adrenaline into his chest and the press of his fingers into his palms.

"Steele," Sean said. "Where do we set up?"

Steele flashed a bright smile. "Over here." He turned and ambled toward a work bench, flipped the wheel locks with his big toe and shoved it

41

back towards the aisles. He was about to move another one but stopped at a row of metal war clubs that had been hung like trophies on the wall. He set his cup down on the table and snatched one of the clubs up. "These are what started me on metal sculpture," and swung the club casually in the air. "Made the first ones in my old garage, you know, for a gimmick." He held it up to his chin. "Shit's fucking heavy," he said. "You could seriously hurt someone if you didn't know what you were doing." He glanced at Zac and smashed the ball end it into the tin cup. The metal crashed and bent as a dark liquid exploded and the sound blasted off the concrete walls. The ring of hard iron faded to echoes in the thick air as the dogs raced for cover and the dark liquid dripped from the table, the walls and Steele's chest.

"So, yeah," Steel said, "just move this shit out of the way."

He left the brutish mace embedded in the cup and headed for a set of iron stairs opposite the entrance. "This is up to the loft," he said and smiled at Kitten who moved not the tiniest of muscles. "I live up here with my fish," he said. "I have a lot of fish."

Kitten couldn't image the horrible sufferings of such fish as had to share a living space with the creature called Steele. He probably talks to them, she thought. He sings them lullabies and calls them his pretty babies. Maybe they have a castle to swim through or a sunken ship with plastic treasure chests. But they can't get out and every morning and every night they have to look at that pock-marked, cut up, sagging flesh mop of a face.

42

"Anyone want to meet the fish?"

"Poor fish," Kitten said.

Steele put one thick finger to the side of his left nostril and blew some snot out of his right. It landed with a wet slap on the concrete floor. He turned to Sean. "You got my stuff?"

"Yeah, man," Sean hustled over to Steele, digging around in his pouch for the baggie and the pain pills in the blue bottle, shoving aside the XTC pills in the brown one.

"Probably need more coke for tonight," Steele snorted. "Can you handle that?"

"Not a problem," Sean said. He handed over the coke and pills. "I'll make a run later. Get a couple more 8-balls."

"Might do it," Steele said and started up the steps, cupping the drugs in his hand.

Sean bounced on his toes. "I'll need some cash," he said.

Steele stopped and turned and looked down at the little dude in his red plaid pants and his red shoes with the white toes and FUCK YOU. He looked over at Raven and then Kitten and then Zac and then back down at Sean.

"You got this right, bro?" he said.

"Dude," Sean said.

"No coke, no party." Steele turned to go up the stairs again.

"I just got you an 8-ball, dude!" Sean hissed up after him.

"Excellent first installment," Steele said and kept on going. "Have two more by tonight or the show's canceled."

Sean's fists tightened into little balls. His lower lip thrust out under the top one. He turned, took two steps, turned back around and then around again. Grit and dirt ground under his rubber soles.

"Oh," Steele called down, "there's more dog shit out there y'all might want to clean up."

Steele laughed and they heard a heavy door open and then slam shut. Zac, Raven and Kitten turned to Sean. He was standing in the middle of the hollow shell, his eyes burning, his arms shaking. In his right hip pocket, Sean carried a butterfly knife. He could whip it out, twirl it around and stab it in a flash of black and silver. He'd practiced the move a hundred thousand times on cantaloupes and sofa cushions and standing there, watching that roided up asshole stomping away, he wanted that knife in his hand and the blade in the guy's neck. But he couldn't do that. His blue-as-the-morning eyes flicked up to Raven.

"Don't worry about it," he said. "Let's get this shit set up." Sean marched out the doors to the car. He slipped a cigarette out of his pouch, tossed his hair to the side and sent the massive flame of the Big Mama lighter against the thin paper and dry weeds and sucked deep.

Raven came out. She gave his shoulder a squeeze and fit her key into the trunk lock. She popped it and stood back. Zac came out and looked inside.

"How did you get a whole drum kit in a trunk?" he said.

Sean spun around and looked up. "Applied spatial dynamics, my man."

Raven slipped the keys onto her belt chain. "Plus," she said, "it's a big fucking trunk."

The band cleared some space, and as Raven began to set up her amp and effects board, and Zac figured out where all his shit went, and Sean began putting together his drum kit, Kitten wandered over to the ring, ran her satin hands over the rough canvas, and thought of men slicing their heads with hidden blades, of fish trapped in transparent cages and getting pinned for a count of three.

4.

The promise of revelry hummed in the blast-furnace air as Raven switched on her amp. Her guitar was lipstick red with a white strap, onto which had been sewn a silk sash that read Miss Teen Texas. Zac watched her adjust it around her shoulders, so it sat like a dress on a wire hanger. She strummed the red pick across the taut metal strings, and the first charge of electric fury issued forth. She tested the pitch of each one, twisted the pegs, and when she was satisfied with the tone and tune, she ripped into the fabric of the sky as her fingers clawed the frets.

A raven moves like black ink through the air, it is liquid, it is ever changing. A raven glides, darts and dives. Ravens chase eagles and crack open robin eggs to devour the unborn. And that is how Raven played her guitar. Her hands moved like liquid while the sound squawked, swooped and soared looking for baby wrens to devour. Zac watched as Raven took flight. She peeled back the clouds and flung them to the asphalt tiled earth. She dove into an ice crusted lake and sent wave upon wave to wreck boats tied to the shore. The guitar was a talisman that connected her to the spiraling forces of the universe, to gravity and dark matter. The Fender

Stratocaster was a being of old, the Morriganne, the Crow, the god that eats the sun every night and craps it out in the morning.

She stopped and twisted the B string.

"Holy fuck." Zac stood with arms hanging, bass hanging, mouth hanging open.

Raven looked up. She passed her pale hand through her bone colored hair. "What?" she said.

"You're amazing," he said.

"Told you," Sean said.

Raven plucked at the D and even that tiny gesture dripped hints of licorice and spice. "Thanks," she mumbled.

Kitten stood in the middle of the ring. She held a notebook in her hand. She looked down at it, at the words she had scribbled between the faint blue lines, at the words she might have said.

"Holy FUCKING MONKEY CRAP!" Steele stomped half-way down the steps. He did a little air guitar riff. "I gotta make a phone call, baby. I know some dudes need to hear you!" He turned to go back up. "Hope the rest of you don't suck!" he said over his shoulder and then he was gone and they heard the door slam.

Zac remembered a football game. His sophomore year at Webster High he'd been named the starting left tackle for the varsity team. His job was to protect the quarterback's blind side and he was good at it. The first six games of the season and he didn't allow a single sack. His coach mentioned some big time college scouts had already been asking about him. Visions of sugarplum Texas cheerleaders danced in his head. Then they played Galveston and Galveston had this kid named Roderick Griffin who played defensive end and had already committed to Oklahoma.

Their first offensive series, as Zac got into his stance and pressed his taped hand into the soft grass, he met Roderick's eyes. They were deep brown eyes off-set by the brilliant whites around them. The dark skin of his cheeks already glistened with sweat. They were not laughing eyes or teasing eyes but eyes lit with the joy of battle. Just before the ball snapped, Roderick smiled. Zac felt his feet turn to lead, his hands to stone, his heart to an origami imitation of a heart. Moments later he was standing in the middle of the field like a big, dumb cow, watching Roderick help his quarterback up off the turf. It had been a moment of profound humility for Zac. He understood that he had just experienced a being beyond him, a man he could not stop, a man who held, within his muscles and nerves, a force he would never touch. Looking at Raven, he felt the same way. He was a cow again, looking up at the sky, watching flight, knowing he would never grow wings.

"Cereal," he said.

"What?" Sean looked up. He had to get his tom-toms adjusted and he was sweating his balls off. He was glad Raven was awesome. It was all coming together, even the drum kit.

Zac plucked the bass. A deep rumbling belched out of the amp. "Someone has to provide the milk," he said.

"Definitely," Sean said. He had no idea what Zac was talking about but wished him well. He was worried about having to go back to Aldo and get more shit. He'd have to ask him to front it to him but he still owed him the money he was supposed to give him from selling Leroy's drums, PA and guitars. He'd sold the two guitars and spent that money on food, a movie and a new t-shirt. The rest of Leroy's stuff was what he and Kitten were using. He was also worried that no one would come tonight even though he'd invited everyone he knew at least twice and he knew a lot of people. He needed to borrow Steele's phone but he also needed to practice because he had only played these drums the one time over at Leroy's until the cops showed up. It was 11:15 and there were elderly neighbors but still, he was just practicing a little. He hadn't played in months, since his first band had busted up and he'd sold his old kit to Jimmy Cleary's little brother but then he'd gone to that poetry reading where Raven had told him to hear Kitten and he was blown away and it just so happened that Leroy was into Aldo for some considerable amounts and was going to give up music anyway and get some technical training, so then all they needed was a bass player and he'd

49

finally thought of Zac but the funniest part was that one of the cops that came knocking on Leroy's garage door was an honest-to-goodness Irish cop and Sean had said, "You're Irish!"

"Yeah," said the cop.

"Me too!" Sean had said.

The cop hardly believed it but they did have the same colored eyes. They might even have been related, Sean pointed out. The cop had said that, well, the Good Lord made the Irish all sorts of ways, didn't he, and to please knock off the racket.

So Sean hadn't practiced much and who knew about Zac and none of them had any idea how well Kitten could sing because she had refused to sing for him. She did write killer poetry though and could really scream it out which was in direct opposition to her performance in bed when she mostly just lay there and mumbled stuff about a bear hitting his head on the stairs. Sean had thought that with all those piercings and all those cuts and burns and everything and the way she teased and tortured, Kitten would be really crazy in bed, but it was like fucking a gunny sack with arms. He should warn Zac about that because it was pretty obvious who her next victim would be. He should also explain that he and Kitten were pretty much not doing it anymore except for last night when he went over to bring her some valium and use her phone. While he was on the phone, trying to get a hold of Zac and calling people about the party she was dropping hot wax on her thighs. One thing led to another but with the valium she was less of a sack and more of Jell-O mold.

Sean secured the toms and sat back down on his stool. Raven was waiting. He picked up his sticks, thumped the bass drum a few times, crashed the high-hat and went on a stomping, smacking, thudding spree. He was the boilermaker, the cranking shaft and the fired core of the earth. He was the thunder and the rain, the mountains falling, the continental tectonics and the last roar of the dinosaurs. He finished with a flourishing crescendo and then looked up.

Raven turned back to her pedal board to check her effects presets.

Zac flipped his amp on, stepped away, threaded the cord around the base of the strap and snapped it in. He pulled a pick out his back pocket, set his right hand to the neck and rested his left on the top of the body. He couldn't think of anything to play or rather he could think of only one thing to play. The song that had no beginning and no end. The last time he'd played it with anybody was the last time he'd seen his brother alive. Just a jam session right before his senior year of high school and he got busy with homework and football. He and James had already talked about the band getting a new bassist because Zac would need to concentrate on school and the band was ready to get really serious, play more gigs in Houston and maybe cut a demo and go on tour. College recruiters were sending letters and making trips to the house and James had already talked to him about making the most of his opportunities and Zac had already mostly gotten over the conflicts of wanting to be in a band, hanging with his brother and maybe going to play in Austin or Dallas in front of a couple dozen kids with maybe going to Austin or Dallas or College Station or Waco or thirty-eight other places to play football in front of 50,000. He'd been reminded of all the crap Lori had gone through to pay for school. But they were done with all that. They had done all that.

It was just him and James and Kurt and the drummer, Dave. Tori wasn't there. Which was unusual. The whole rehearsal had been unusual. James and Kurt usually played right next to each other, singing in the same mic most of the time but that night they'd kept their distance and Kurt hadn't joined in on the vocals. That had been the night Dave said he'd gotten some girl pregnant and he'd brought a bottle of Jack to celebrate. That night they played that one song until Dave fell over asleep behind his kit and they had to leave the boat storage unit they used unlocked for fear they might forget about him in the morning.

Kurt and James usually rode together but that night Kurt drove off in his truck by himself and James had his own car there.

Zac had asked his brother what was going on.

"Nothing, man," James had said. "Nothing."

The nothing went on and on, on and on, like the deep blue sounds of the universe stretching out.

"Hey, Sean!" Steele said. Zac hadn't heard the door open or the flip-flop flapping feet come half-way down the stairs.

"What?" Sean said.

"You remember what I said about hoping the rest of you didn't suck," he said.

"Yeah?" Sean said.

"You suck!" Steele laughed. "You playing a fucking funeral there, big guy? What the fuck!" He laughed again and then pointed at Raven. "You keep rocking, baby!" He gave her a thumbs up and went back his loft.

Sean stared blazing lasers at the tightly pulled skin of the snare.

"Maybe," said Raven to him, "you could just play a simple beat so Zac can get a groove."

Sean looked up at Raven. She was just the whole world with her guitar, he thought. Take that away and she was a skeleton on Prozac. He turned to Zac.

"I didn't realize I was playing," Zac said.

"It was a lot like playing," Sean snapped. His eyes did a zigzag up and down Zac. He really did look like a bassist. He might need to take Zac along to Aldo's. In the meantime, he needed Zac to play like a mother-fucking-rock-and-roll-punk-out-crazy-ass bassist and not just look like one. "Right," he said. "When I was a kid all I wanted to do was thunder across the plains like the massive herds of buffalo that used to roam the west

53

because when I was a kid I always had to be one of the Indians when we played cowboys and Indians, me and these two Mexican kids, because we were the only kids with brown skin. One of those kids used to bawl his fucking eyes out because he wanted to be a cowboy. He even brought pictures of Mexican cowboys to show us but we still made him be an Indian because everyone knows cowboys were white and Indians were dark and anyway it's the Indians that get to chase buffalo, steal women and scalp white men. The cowboys just get to eat beans and fuck their horses. So right now, we all need to be Indians on a war path. Got it?"

"I'll get it," said Zac.

"Good," said Sean.

Raven shook out her arms and rolled her head around her neck. "What song are we doing?"

Sean popped his knuckles. "Let's do that song we didn't use to do."

"Okay," Raven said. She looked up at Zac. "Just play the root when you feel it."

Zac nodded and lowered his head. He watched his fingers flex.

"Hey, Kitten!" Sean called out. "You gonna join us?"

"I'm musing!" She yelled without looking up. She'd sat down in the corner of the ring. She looked like she was writing in her journal but she

54

was actually drawing little pictures of little arrows sticking out of a flock of dead birds.

"Whatever," said Sean with a double foot stomp. "Hey, you think we should play naked like those Chili Pepper guys?"

"No," Raven said.

Sean shrugged. It had been an idea.

The idea returned to Sean as he set his sticks on the snare and released the catch because after two hours of rehearsing they still pretty much sucked. Zac was too slow, Sean was too fast and Raven kept going too far out there. They'd managed to get two short original pieces mashed together, plus the Green Eggs and Ham song pretty well down but, it was like they were all riding bicycles down the same hill and one of them kept putting on his brakes, the other one had no brakes and the girl kept doing double back flips off of parked cars and trashcan lids.

The morning had crawled towards noon and heat of the day had filled the warehouse. They were like a slow-cooking crock pot full of ribs, the meat dripping off their bones. Kitten had slid down from the ring and wandered into the stacks of scrap metal. She'd found a large rusted drum to curl up in and didn't come out until they stopped playing and Sean sparked up a joint.

"We need to keep practicing," Raven said.

"I'm hungry." Zac set the bass down against the amp. A loud squawk emanated until he cut the power. "Sorry."

"We need a break." Sean squatted on the floor, the joint smoldering between his dark brown fingers. In what Houston called winter, his skin faded to a shade like a muslin screen but in the dregs of summer, he was a deep nut brown. He was a seasonal creature, like an arctic fox. "We'll hit the Ristorante Mexicana on the way to Aldo's."

"Who's Aldo?" Zac asked.

Sean stood up. "Well, he used to be this kid named Frank that was a couple years ahead of me in high school but now…," he passed the joint to Zac. "He's the man," he said and looked out the open bay doors and into the sizzling air.

5.

Raven looked up from her nachos as Zac shoveled a fork full of

beef enchilada into his mouth. The spice flecked red sauce splashed against

his chin as the ground beef was macerated between his teeth and the tortilla

slithered down his throat. He'd ordered the full plate with beans and rice

and was almost done. During football season days, he could have put away

three of those plates, but it had been some time since then and his appetite

was not what it once was. The last few days he'd gotten by on cigarettes,

bologna sandwiches and a 2 liter bottle of Diet Coke but now he was

hungry.

Zac watched Kitten eat one chicken taco and start on her second.

She had said she could eat anything but her favorite thing to eat was Thai

red curry with tofu and vegetables because the tofu soaked up the curry the

best. She had added completely unnecessarily that it gave her diarrhea for

days but she loved it so what was she going to do? She had gone vegan for

a month once but kept slipping up and having cottage cheese with avocado

mixed in. Every now and then she would go on a cooking tear and make cakes, pies or a pot roast. She had been talking and talking and talking even as she picked a piece of lettuce out of her lip piercings.

As she went on about falafel Zac glanced over at Sean. He watched him stirring his iced tea, testing it, adding another half-packet of sugar, stirring, testing again and finally satisfied, draining as much of it as he could as quickly as he could before the attentive waitress ambled by to refill it again and throw off the whole sugar-to-tea-gastromolecular balance. He was halfway through his Burrito El Supremo but kept getting sidetracked by the chips and salsa.

Kitten had moved on to the delights of peanut butter and mayonnaise sandwiches as Raven took a sip of her super-sweetened iced tea, touched the edge of a nacho and lifted it up with her finger. the cheese had congealed so half the pile rose with it and she put it back. She took another sip of her iced tea and put her hands in her lap. She lifted her head and stared out the window. Zac shoveled another bite and turned his head. Across the street, beyond a chain link fence, a dozen or so Hispanic kids were scrambling around on the school yard playground. They were yelling and laughing, running and falling, crying and getting over it.

"You need to eat," Sean said.

Zac looked back at the table. Raven slumped back into the corner of the booth, her fingers picked at the corner of a chip.

"You need your energy for tonight."

"I know," she said. She cracked off a corner and placed it in her mouth so as to avoid her black smeared lips.

Zac took one of the last chips from the basket and scooped up the remnants of beans, rice and sauce left on his plate.

Sean shifted his hips and leaned forward, his blue eyes dancing with glee. "That was pretty hot about having sex in the sky," he said.

Kitten shook her head. There was a faint tinkling sound. "You're gross," she said.

"What?" He gave his tea three stirs. "Two chicks together are hot and if one of them has a raven head and they're falling through the air doing a double-barrel sixty-nine, that's double plus hot." He took a long slurp.

Raven pried loose a whole nacho. "It was just a dream," she said.

Zac slurped down the last sauce-dripping chip. "I had a dream once where my brother came back to the house. He had a garbage bag full of stuff that he wanted me to keep for him." Zac used his finger to get the very last smudge of sauce on the plate. "When he left I opened up the bag. It was full of frogs."

"Dead frogs?" Kitten said.

"No," Zac replied. "Live ones. They were hopping all over." He slurped his finger clean.

"I hate frogs." She shook herself and jingled. She nodded at Zac. "You have sauce on your chin."

59

Zac grabbed a stained and crumpled paper napkin from the table and wiped his chin. He looked at the napkin. It looked like smeared blood.

"What would be your animal name, Zac?" Sean turned his head to the big guy.

Zac put the napkin down. He took a sip of his Diet Coke. "In high school I got called Donkey."

The waitress rumbled by and before Sean could stop her she'd refilled his tea, smiled a broad, friendly smile and then frowned as Raven covered her own glass with her skeletal hands and shook her head. The waitress shrugged and moved back to the front counter where her mother or aunt or sister was folding napkins.

"Gracias," mumbled Sean. He grabbed another small pile of sugar packets. "Donkey?"

"Yeah," Zac said.

"Why Donkey?" Sean said.

Zac glanced out the window at the kids whispering secrets into each other's ears and then running to tell the others. "Just stubborn, I guess." He shoved his hand into his shorts pocket and clawed out his smokes. "Y'all mind?"

Kitten shook her head and took another bite of her taco. She told Zac one of her biggest thrills when she was four was to light her father's Lucky Strikes for him. Zac said he used to do the same thing for both his parents. Then Kitten had mentioned how, of course, that was before her father started raping her and how she shot him with his own gun when she was eleven which put a damper on the conversation.

Raven folded her hands in her lap again. Now she definitely couldn't eat. Not with smoke flopping out at her and Kitten telling her abused childhood stories. She didn't mind the stories as much as the smoke. She'd tried cigarettes a number of times. A girl named Darcy, who she'd see at almost every pageant, would sneak her mom's Virginia Slims and they'd smoke them on the balcony of the hotel while their moms were down at the bar, but Raven never really liked them or ever wanted another one. When she started working at Nan's Records a guy named Spencer turned her on to cloves. They tasted sweet, she didn't have to inhale them and she could take smoke breaks out by the dumpster like everyone else. She placed her napkin over the nachos and dragged her cigarette case out of the bag at her feet. She popped the case open and slid out one of the long, black sticks.

"I want to be called Snake!" Sean said. "But not just any snake. A specific snake, like King Cobra or Death Adder." Kitten almost choked on the last bite of her taco as snorts and chuckles shuddered through her. Her eyes began to water with trying to keep the food from going down the wrong way. "What?"

"You're so not a snake. Maybe a gerbil or something. Maybe a hamster like the kind perverts stick up their butts."

Sean threw a piece of tomato at her. Kitten retaliated with a guacamole covered shred of chicken. Zac stared down at his plate, at the swirls of red sauce and little chunky bits.

"We're going to suck tonight," Raven said. "I don't know if I want to do this." She took a drag of her clove, let the smoke roll out of her mouth and twist up into her nose before being expelled again.

Sean watched her. He glanced over at Kitten and then looked back at Raven. She met his eyes briefly then dropped them down to her barely touched plate. He leaned forward. "We're going to rock," he said.

Raven glanced over at Zac who was still swirling around and around and around.

"I don't know how you can say that," she said.

"I can say that," Sean said, "because that's what's going to happen." He pulled out a smoke from the pack Zac left on the table. "We're going to go back and really fucking practice and fucking rock." He borrowed the Zippo too, snapped it open and clicked the flame. His face scrunched up as he lit his cigarette. "I can't stand that taste you get with a Zippo," he said, turning to face Zac. "That lighter fluid taste, you know?"

"We need more practice than a few hours," Raven said.

Sean looked back at her. "We will. This is just a party. It's just to get us started."

Raven sat up, twirled the clove in her boney fingers and slumped back the other way. "I just don't want it to be like last time."

"It won't," Sean said.

"How can you say that?"

"Look at me," Sean said. "Raven, look at me."

Raven lifted her mahogany eyes to meet Sean's endless horizon and their promise of the edge of the world.

"It won't."

Raven closed her eyes and took another drag. In the sweet numbing substance that filled her mouth she tasted the hours wasted waiting for a singer to show, a bassist to go buy a new string and a drummer to pack a bowl.

She sat up, folded the arms that attached to her shoulders over each other and let her hair drape over her face. "I just don't want to be the only one who gives a shit," she said.

Sean tapped some ash onto his plate. "Raven..."

Kitten's little hands balled themselves up into little fists. "I give a shit."

As Raven lifted her head, the bleached-out hair that shrouded her face fell away. "I hope so," she said. "Because it takes...I wake up, I

63

practice, I go to work, I come home and I practice. That's what it takes. It takes hours and hours every day. We can't..."

"This is just the first day," Sean said.

"I am going to give a shit!" Kitten said.

"You wouldn't rehearse with us," Raven said.

"I will!"

"When?"

"When I am fucking ready, Raven!"

"It's just a goddamn party," Sean said twice.

"It shouldn't be." Raven poked a cracked fingernail at Sean. "It shouldn't just be a goddamn party like those goddamn parties we played last time."

"Raven's right," Zac said.

"Raven needs to eat her lunch and get a fucking life." Kitten folded her arms and stared daggers down at the floor.

Zac mashed out his cigarette in a green ashtray. "I can walk home from here," he said. "I'll pick up my amp another time. Or you can keep it." He looked up at Raven. "Just need to get the bass out of the car."

"I'll give you a ride," Raven said.

"I bet you will," Kitten spat.

"What the fuck is your problem?"

"What the fuck do you think is my problem?"

64

"How the fuck should I know?"

"Stop," Sean said.

"Because I tell you everything!"

"You tell everybody everything! It's like this constant deluge of Kitten's worst nightmares!"

"STOP!"

Everyone stopped. Raven stopped and Kitten stopped. Zac sat back down. The women folding napkins stopped folding napkins. The three men in the corner stopped talking in Spanish. The mom in the booth stopped trying to get her three year old to eat his beans and his sister stopped slurping her orange soda. They all waited for Sean to say something next.

The cigarette in Sean's hand trembled over the ash-speckled plate. He pressed his other hand flat to the table. His eyes were shut. His teeth set hard against each other. When he spoke, his voice was careful, measured and quiet. The women went back to their napkins, the men back to their conversation, the mother back to her children and the children back to their delightful games.

"We all need this," he said. "Raven, you need a band. We need to be that band if you'll let us. Kitten needs a place to scream. Zac needs a reason to live. I need a way out. I can't cancel the gig. I've already called, like, a thousand people and...let's just do this tonight and tomorrow I'll find us a practice space and we'll practice every day. I promise." He looked up at Raven. "It won't be like last time. I swear on my mother's life."

"You don't talk to your mother," Raven mumbled.

"I'm half-Irish so that's a big swear regardless and I'm pretty sure Vietnamese are big into mom swears too so…so look…" He turned to Kitten and then Zac. "We stop at Aldo's which will only take five minutes and then we head back to the warehouse and we put in some hours and get that shit tight…"

Raven's eyes rolled to the upper right.

"As tight as we can get it and we just rock out and get serious tomorrow, okay? Is that a deal? Are we in? Is Double Murder Suicide going to live or die?"

Kitten swiped a cigarette from Zac's pack that was still sitting on the table. "That totally didn't make sense." She used her own lighter.

"You know what I mean," Sean said.

Kitten blew out an expansive cloud. "I do. I'm in."

Zac considered his dwindling supply of cigarettes and recalled his first. He had been born in smoke and swaddled in ash but had never put the tar to his own lips until that day when he walked in on death's gruesome tableau. He found a pack of Camel Lights on the kitchen counter. He didn't know if they belonged to Kurt or his brother. It didn't matter. He lit one with shaking hands. He coughed and shook and cried. It was all a matter of

66

when the end would come and how many bodies would litter the ditches along the road.

"I'm in," he said.

Sean put a hand on his shoulder and grinned. He turned to Raven.

The waitress sidled by, collected the plates and left the check.

Raven carefully mashed out the end of the clove. She put the remainder back in her silver cigarette case. She looked out the window, at the kids across the street. She remembered those times when she got to run and play and wish the sun would stay up five minutes more.

"Okay," she said.

6.

Kitten eyed the oak-shaded street as Raven found a space big

enough for her Buick. They were over near the art museum. Thirties-era

houses were interspersed with two-story apartment complexes, everything

sharing a deep wood colored tone. They were a block away from the Pine

Crest Apartment complex that Sean said Aldo lived in. He had told Raven

to just pull up to the gate and he'd have Aldo buzz them in and she could

park in the one of the visitor's spots but Kitten had nixed that idea.

"I don't want to be trapped," she had said.

Sean had pleaded from the back seat where Zac was still practicing.

He'd been practicing since they left the Mexican place. He'd brought the

bass along with the idea of practicing but figured it would remain an idea

but after what Sean had said and Raven had said he'd been going all out to

get used to the old sensations. He was getting there, inch by inch, but he

was having to think about where to slide his weakened fingers and having to

think about which forgotten string to pluck.

Raven had said, "There's never enough room in those places," and rolled down the street until she found a space and with the greatest of precision wedged the beast back and forth until it rested in its berth.

Kitten snapped a spent cigarette out the window, into the snarled green yard beyond the sidewalk. "Leave space so we can get away quick."

Raven put the car in park and turned off the ignition. "Baby doesn't do anything quick, Kitten," she said.

It seemed cooler in this part of town, with all the oak trees bending low over the street, their roots buckling the sidewalks and pushing against the curbs. Kitten sat up and looked up the street and down. She opened her door and popped out, one black boot still in the car, one hand on the door, one on the roof, twisting her head back and forth, snapping glances at the sky.

Sean got out. "What are you doing?"

"I'm looking for unmarked cars or surveillance vans or helicopters."

Sean looked down the street. Dappled sunlight carpeted the asphalt and the roofs of the dull-colored cars. He looked the other way and shut his door.

"Fucking relax, Kitten," Sean said. "Yo, Zac, c'mon."

Zac held a low hum then let it die. "Okay," he said. He popped the door and got out, dragging the bass along with him.

69

"If y'all aren't back in five minutes we're gone," Kitten said. She ducked back in the car and shut the door.

Sean adjusted the pack he wore on his hip and leaned towards the window. "Could you do me a favor, Kitten?"

"What?"

"Make it ten, in case I have to take a dump or something?" Sean smiled and turned and led Zac up the street.

"You're gross!" Kitten called after him in a sing-song way. She dug in her purse for another cigarette but her mouth was starting to taste like tar so she shoved the purse back into the seat "Do you have a mint or something?" she asked Raven.

"Yeah," Raven said and took her eyes away from the mirror. She'd been watching Zac join Sean and thinking how funny they looked together, the big guy and the little guy. Such a classic juxtaposition, she thought and then stuffed her hand down into her bag. It wasn't hard to find a pack of gum. There were three or four of them in there to cover her bile-tainted breath. She thought she might want one too so she pulled out two sticks and handed one to Kitten and slid one out for herself.

Kitten took the gum, unwrapped it and tossed the wrapper out the window where it fell and fluttered on the sidewalk. The heat rolled in from the freeways, rolled over the rows of houses and covered every crevice of the human body. Raven pulled at her shirt, fanning herself with it. Kitten

70

kept staring down the street. She kept turning and looking behind her. She made a yuk face and spat the gum out the window. It landed on the sidewalk, right where someone should step on it, and this made Kitten happy for a flicker of time, but then she looked out the front window, at the blue car in front of her and the cars parked in parade down the street.

"Spearmint gum gives me headaches," she said.

"Sorry," Raven said. "I have others."

"Do you have the flavor burster kind?"

"No."

Kitten folded her hands in her lap. "Never mind."

"Sorry."

"Me too," she said. "I mean about what I said at lunch. I'm sorry. I know it's hard."

Raven bit her lip and then stopped. She was a lip biter from when she was just a little kid and her mom was always on her about it, so that's why she always stopped. Every time she bit her lip, she heard her mother's voice in her head telling her to stop, telling her she'd ruin her lovely smile which is the key to winning and everything else. The whole world could be hers with just the right glossy smile. The memories compacted together so tightly, so familiar, so understood. A bite of the lip and then stop. A lifetime of experience in the sensation of teeth on skin.

"It is," she said.

Kitten turned and opened her arms. Raven leaned over and they embraced, Kitten's smile wide and arms crushing. Raven's hold was loose but her fingers found the small of Kitten's back, touching the soft skin and slick sweat. Kitten slid her arms up to Raven's neck and darted a quick kiss to Raven's lips. Raven's arms held in the air like pine branches.

Kitten tilted her head forward, drowning Raven in wide almond eyes. Her lips parted again, the dappled light danced over the silver jewels. "Don't you wish you had a tank," she said. "Then we could crush all these cars. And when the cops come, we could just blow their asses up." Kitten tilted herself back, letting her arms fall to her side, letting Raven sit back up.

"I'll look into it."

"Maybe a monster truck," Kitten said.

"That would be cool." Raven wiped her hand across her sweating brow and decided to finish the half-smoked clove cigarette from lunch. "The Double Murder Suicide Monster Truck."

"What do you think of that name? For a band?"

Raven removed the gum from her mouth and placed it in the foil-like wrapper and then put the wrapper in her bag before sliding out the cigarette case. "Better than the last one. Plastic Jesus."

Kitten hopped up on her knees, turned around then turned back. "Where the fuck are they?"

Raven opened the case, caught the waft of sweet aroma and pulled out the half-smoked one. "It's only been a minute."

"Do you think Zac's okay with that name? I mean, I don't know if I would be. What do you think of Zac?" Kitten said.

"He's working on it," Raven said.

"Not as a musician," Kitten said. "Would you sleep with him?"

"He wouldn't want to," she said.

"Oh course he wants to," Kitten said. "They all want to. Do you want to?"

Raven pictured her skeletal frame beneath Zac's sheer size and wondered what it would be like to get crushed under the weight. "I don't know," she said.

"Well," Kitten said, "We're in a band now. We'll probably all sleep together at some point." Kitten dropped her head to her chest and smoothed out the fabric of her tartan skirt with her satin gloves. At some point in the next few hours she was going to have to sing, but it was like there was a stop in her throat. Half a dozen times, while Zac and Sean and Raven were practicing, she made to join them but her throat seized up on her, just seized up and made her feet turn back. She looked out the front window. She took a quick peek out the back. She looked over at Raven and put a hand on her thigh. At one of her foster homes, Kitten had found a dead crow. She'd picked it up and was surprised at how light it was and how much the feathers concealed the tiny bones beneath. Touching Raven was a lot like touching a raven.

"You're going to have so many groupies," she said.

"Not me." Raven lit her clove and held the smoke in her mouth, letting just the tiniest bit seep down into her lungs. It filled her up some. Her stomach complained of its emptiness. She would really like some cake. "You will."

"No thank you," Kitten said. "And I'm not sleeping with Sean anymore." She gave Raven's thigh another pat and then moved her hand back to her lap. "He keeps trying to stick his finger in my butt. God, it's like those doctors. You remember those doctors?"

"Yeah." It was the day she woke up. She was thirteen and she'd woken up in a hospital bed with a cast on her leg and an IV dripping nutrients into her blood, next to a girl with a pierced nose and bandages on her arms. The girl said her name was Kitten and any minute now a doctor would come in and stick a thermometer up her butt and she was right.

"You ever have a guy try to stick his finger in your butt?" Kitten said.

Raven winced as a branch was brushed aside by a breeze and a shot of sunlight dazzled her. "No. I don't have that much experience," she said. The breeze blew another way and the sunlight was cut off. "I'm a virgin, actually, if you want to know the truth."

74

"What!" Kitten spun around and climbed up on her knees.

"Yes," said Raven.

"How did that happen?"

"I don't know. It just didn't." She took a drag of her clove.

"You never told me!"

"You never asked."

"Have you ever seen a penis?"

"Yes," Raven said, dusting ash off her leg. She'd seen her father's penis from when she was little and she would sometimes watch him pee and ask him why he had that silly thing and why he put it in every ditch from Texas to New York, which was what mommy said. She never got a good answer. She'd also seen Harlen Stewart's penis. He was the host for the Junior Miss Teen Contest in Kerville and she'd accidently opened the wrong door and caught him tugging on it.

"Ever almost?"

"A few times."

"Sean?"

"No."

"Really?"

Raven shrugged.

Kitten edged toward her. "Four years we've known each other and you never told me you're a virgin."

Raven thought that strictly speaking this was true. They had met in that hospital and then a year later Kitten had called her up out of the blue and asked her if she wanted to go to a Cure concert. Raven had been enthralled by how Robert Smith could wrap an entire arena inside the spidery tendrils of his guitar work. Kitten couldn't have given a fuck; she just wanted to get backstage. Somehow they did and somehow she ended up asking Robert Smith how he got that wailing crunching sound. He talked to her about reverb and echo, gave a quick lesson on acoustics and told her to practice day and night. By then, Kitten had disappeared and would not be seen again until two years later when Raven started working at Nan's Records and, a week after that, Kitten started there too.

"What happened to you that night at the Cure concert?"

"Same old shit."

They spent hours and hours together since then, stocking CD's and t-shirts, yelling at punk-ass little shoplifters, coming up with top ten lists and taking smoke breaks out by the dumpster. Kitten came to a couple of the old band's shows. She might have had something to do with the singer OD'ing. She started writing poetry. Raven had listened.

Raven pulled in a mouthful of smoke and glanced at the side mirror. Two blocks away a white van stopped at the intersection.

"We're just going to have to do something about that," Kitten said. She twisted and turned. The van had moved on. 'Where the fuck are those guys?"

"There's one thing you need to know about Aldo," Sean said just before he knocked on the dark brown apartment door.

"What's that?" Zac said.

Sean knocked. "His two favorite movies are *Scarface* and *Rocky Horror Picture Show*. You do the math."

Zac shook his head. The calculations were boggling. It was like the Astronomy course he didn't drop and the stellar parallax.

"Oh," Sean said, "and he's got this big, giant Mexican dude named Manny that works for him. Don't mention the Jose Cruz thing."

"What Jose Cruz thing?"

Sean put a finger to his lips to shush him as the door opened. For Zac it was like opening a door and meeting a brick wall except the wall was the big, giant Mexican dude. Manny was only an inch or so taller but he was twice as wide and it was a rare sensation for Zac to suddenly feel small, to feel the oppression of a massive black t-shirt, the weight of a big silver cross around a neck the size of a pumpkin and to have to look up to see his own puny reflection in the mirrored sunglasses beneath a thick mat of hair.

"Yo, Manny," Sean said and held out his hand. "This is my boy, Zac. He's cool."

Manny engulfed Sean's hand in his own and brought the little guy in for a bro-hug. He released him and held out his hand to Zac.

"S'up," he said.

Zac slung the bass behind him and held out his own. He watched as it was made to disappear. He could almost have forgotten he had a hand until he felt his finger bones being crushed together. Manny let Zac's hand fall and stood aside from the doorway. He wore jean shorts so long they ended just above a massive pair of unlaced Jordan's. "Aldo's upstairs," he said to Sean and offered the two boys entry to the apartment.

"I'll just be a few minutes," Sean said over his shoulder to Zac and sprinted up the stairs. Zac held his bass at his side and stepped into the living room. It was remarkably cool, clean and orderly. A black leather couch faced a glass coffee table, with two black leather chairs opposite. A black bookshelf with spaces for a TV, VCR, Nintendo, CD rack and stereo system occupied the entire wall. The hardwood floors had been stained as near to black as near can get with a white carpet between the shelves and the sofa that was the texture of the fluffy snow Zac remembered falling on the early-January day that his family left Boston, even though they told him he was too young to remember it. Beyond the living room, he saw a kitchen which featured black countertops and white shelves. On the walls there were five movie posters. All five of them were of Tony Montoya shooting a large gun, holding a large gun, looking like he was about to shoot a large gun, surrounded by cocaine and large guns or sitting in a bubble bath.

"Have a seat," Manny said, indicating one of the chairs.

Zac sat, pulling the bass onto his lap.

Manny reached under his canopied shirt and extracted a 9 mm from whatever fold he might have wedged it under and sat down on the couch, placing the gun with a clank on the glass as he did so. He leaned back and put his arm up on the back of the sofa. The barrel of the gun was pointing directly at Zac. It was just like the gun he'd found on his brother's blood-soaked floor.

"You all right, bro?" Manny asked.

Zac could hear the cool air blowing through a vent in the wall. He could feel his sweat turning cold. He could see himself reflected in the mirrored sunglasses. Two tiny versions of himself. "You ever meet anyone bigger than you?"

"Oh, yeah," Manny said. His face folded into a smile.

Kitten had been tapping her fingers on the rim of the open window, alternating the clink of the chrome on the outside with the thump of leather within. She would glance first down the street in front of her and then into the side mirror she'd adjusted to see behind. Nothing moved or stirred except the sweat that beaded on her lip and rolled down her spine. She lifted her butt off the seat, leaning forward on her hands. She turned her head to Raven with dramatic flourish and seductive style bent. "Ever been with a girl?"

"No," Raven said. She accidently inhaled the clove smoke and started choking. She had to thump her thin chest with the heel of her palm and brace the other hand against the steering wheel before she could continue. "Sort of."

Kitten slid her tongue piercing along her lip until it tapped the rings in the corners. Raven drew breath in a rattle, looked at Kitten and then looked away and then down at the ash smudge on her leg. "At the Junior Texas Rose pageant in San Antonio, when I was thirteen, my friend Darcy and I watched *The Hunger*."

"Love that movie," whispered Kitten.

Raven looked up. Kitten was rising up on her haunches and she could see down the deep hanging cleft between her breasts. She looked back down at her leg. "Our moms were at the hotel bar."

"Of course they were." Kitten swished her rump around. "Did you and Darcy make out?"

Raven's white cheeks flushed a blotchy red. Kitten drew a delighted gasp.

"Did you and Darcy touch each other?"

Raven nodded her head.

"Did you…"

"That's all we did," Raven said.

"Did you like it?"

Raven turned her head. Kitten's metal crusted face was inches from her own. She gave Kitten a quick peck on the nose. "We were just kids. The movie ended and our moms would be up soon."

Kitten sighed a warming hum, flipped over, lowered her head onto Raven's lap and stretched out. Her feet barely touched the passenger door. She looked up at Raven with soft wide eyes.

"What are you doing?" Raven said.

The heat that filled the car was even thicker and more oppressive down below the steering wheel. Raven's black pants were coarse and heavy. She longed for something smooth and silky to rub against. "Do you shave your legs?" she said.

"I shave everything," Raven said.

"Everything?"

"Yup." Raven was holding her arms out, like her namesake balancing on a wire. She finally dropped her left arm, the one holding the clove, onto the open window and let her right fall onto Kitten's thigh. "Why do you ask?"

"Just wondering."

81

"Wondering what?"

Kitten rolled her head this way and that. The car smelled of polishers and cleaner scents. Raven smelled like yesterday. "What it would be like to get to choose my first time. I think that might have made a real difference."

"With what?" Raven asked.

"Oh, everything," Kitten purred and rubbed her head across Raven's thighs and smiled.

From this angle, when Kitten talked, Raven thought, it was like a machine was moving its mouth parts because of all the piercings, and it took some doing, some staring to see how soft and pretty she really was. "How far do you think we'll go? Are we really in a band? I know we just said we are but did we just say it because that's the sort of thing you say on a Saturday? Will Zac really kill himself? Will you ever get laid? Will Sean ever shut up? How come I don't smile when I see a puppy?"

Raven laughed. "Because puppies have sharp little dagger teeth and they pee on your shoes," she said. She took a drag of the clove cigarette and slid her hand down Kitten's leg, from the scratchy tartan fabric to the slick black tights as she blew the smoke out the window.

Sean found Aldo standing naked in the bathroom sliding a sleek silver razor up the olive colored skin of his neck. His body was lean and smooth, his buttocks firm and his cock uncircumcised. As he lifted his pointed chin and stared down his angular face it wobbled in moist and fragrant air.

"Looking good, Aldo." Sean leaned against the doorway.

"How do you shave, Sean?" His voice was like oil, like a sound that has always been there but went unnoticed. "Do you go up or down?"

"I don't really have to shave much," Sean said.

"But when you do?"

Sean laughed a little bit. Aldo was always pretending he was in a movie, or maybe he wasn't pretending. Sean sometimes wondered if Aldo's world was colored by gels and recorded by boom mics. "I don't know, Aldo. From up to down, I guess."

"Always draw the blades upwards, do you see," Aldo said as he drew the blade up, against the grain of the hair, shaving it clean.

"Yeah, that's good advice, Aldo," Sean said.

"Yes, it is," Aldo said.

"You're a lefty" Manny said to Zac.

"Yeah," Zac said. He supposed the bass was a dead giveaway.

"You practicing?"

"Yeah," Zac said. "We're playing a party tonight."

"Oh," Manny said. "Show me."

83

Zac looked back down at the bass and then back up.

"I'm pretty rusty," he said.

"That's okay. I like music." Manny smiled.

"It's not plugged in."

"That's okay, bro." Zac could feel the sweat running down his ribs. Manny waggled a fat finger. "Go ahead."

Zac glanced at the gun and the man sitting behind it. He lifted the bass to rest on his legs and fished out the pick from his pocket. He placed his fingers on the neck like and started to pluck. He tried doing one of the new songs, the second new song, the one he was supposed to start but he soon found himself slowing down, surrounded by gray smoke and the fogs of memories he couldn't brush away.

Manny nodded along. Zac was reminded of Jabba the Hutt rocking out in his lair which made him laugh just a little and lose the beat. He tried to get it back but now his fingers were fumbling about and he had to stop, start over...get lost...look at his fingers...

"Yo," Manny said.

Zac looked up.

"Play that thing."

"I am."

"You ain't! You're just picking at it. Give me that shit!" Manny reached out his thick arm and Zac placed the bass in his catcher's mitt sized

84

hand. Manny swung it onto his expansive lap and began slapping and thumping at it as his fingers glided and dance. The strings twanged and vibrated with his percussive attentions. He stopped. "This upside down shit is weird," he said.

Zac shrugged.

"The bass is like the heartbeat, bro." Manny handed Zac the instrument back. "You got to bring the beat to that shit." He raised his hands in front of him and busted out some moving and shaking which made the whole massive mound of himself quiver and quake which made the couch shutter which made the entire apartment complex tremble. "That bass gets thumping BOOM BOOM BOOM! That's the heartbeat, bro! The bass thumps and everyone's heart starts to pound, yo!" If Manny had been in Lake Conroe, tidal waves would be crushing boat houses. "The bass stops," Manny said and his great bulk came to a shivering, quivering rest. "The heart stops," he said. He lowered his hands, he leaned back, he put his arm back on the back of the couch and then he pointed at Zac and said, "Keep that heart pumping, bro."

Zac felt the thickness of the strings under his fingertips and the effort it took to snap the pick across them.

At a certain point, Sean realized the human capacity to watch another human do a routine task was limited.

"Hey, Aldo, can I use your phone?"

Aldo set the razor down. He lifted a white hand towel from the side of the sink and pressed it to his face. He pulled it away and turned his attention to Sean.

"Why?"

Sean shuffled his feet. He watched his feet shuffling. "I just have to call some people about the party tonight."

"Your band." Aldo put the towel down.

Sean looked up. "Yeah."

Aldo let slip a long, slow breath. Sean remembered ninth grade soccer practice. He was a freshman trying to make the varsity team. He ran fast and tackled hard. After sliding into a ball and knocking it away from one of the juniors he stood up and found himself facing a boy staring down at him with eyes like polished oak.

"Don't do that again," the boy had said.

"Fuck you," Sean had replied.

The boy let slip a long slow breath and kicked him in the nuts. Sean never tried to tackle Aldo again.

Aldo nodded and Sean went into the big bedroom at the front of the apartment, and sat on Aldo's big, black satin bed and picked up the phone. He called Carmen and left a message on her machine, saying he was at his friend's place who had a mirror on the ceiling over his bed, and how cool

86

that was when you thought about it. He also reminded her to come to the party and bring her friends and he'd have lots of stuff on him.

He hung up just before Aldo came in. Aldo had an odd way of walking. His feet seemed to grip at the carpet. It seemed entirely plausible that he could simply turn and walk up the wall if he wanted to. He did not do this. He went to his black-stained dresser, slid open the second drawer from the top and pulled out a pair of red silk panties. He regarded these a moment and then pulled them on, adjusting himself until he was comfortable.

"I like those, Aldo," Sean said.

"Was it your mother or father who was a gook?" Aldo said

A worm threaded its way through Sean's belly. "My dad."

"And your mother is Irish," Aldo said.

"Aye, laddy," Sean said in his best impression of the Lucky Charms leprechaun. Something was doing a little jig on his spine.

"Did kids ever call you Rice Paddy?"

"Actually, yes," Sean said. "You remember Ryan Tanner?"

"I knew his brother," Aldo said.

"Nick, yeah. Two assholes." Sean said.

"Indeed." Aldo went to his closet, opened the doors and went in.

Sean perched himself on the edge of the bed. "It was in Mr. Lippert's class. During lab. He kept going, 'Hey Rice Paddy', 'Want some frog guts, Rice Paddy?' I finally...I picked up my bio book and clocked him. Mr. Lippert, I mean he had to send me to Mrs. Eisenhower's office but he was laughing when he did it." Sean's leg began to pump up and down. "That kid was always busting on Mr. Lippert."

Aldo returned from the closet with white pants that did not completely cover the fact that he was wearing red panties. He passed a hand through his dark brown hair. He was a picture of bored elegance, the kind you buy in a store already framed. He sat down next to Sean.

"Do you speak Vietnamese?" he said.

"No."

"Why not?"

"I grew up here," Sean said. "With my mom."

"Where's your dad?"

Sean shifted his hip pack around to the front and then over to the other side. "Fuck if I know. California, I think. I only met him once."

"You met him?" Aldo smelled of leathery spice with floral hints.

"Yeah," Sean said. He wanted to scoot over but there was no room to scoot. He was trapped by the headboard on one side and Aldo on the other. "I came home from school..."

"What year were you?" Aldo said. His smooth face was turned completely to Sean, his eyes digging for something.

88

"Eighth," Sean said. Trying not to look away and then looking away.

"Go on," Aldo said.

"I came home and there was this black car in the driveway with diplomatic plates. That's what they said on them and there was a guy in a black suit standing at our door. When I got up to him he asked me who I was. I told him I lived there and he said something into a little microphone in his sleeve."

"Really?"

"Yeah," Sean said, starting to bounce a bit. "Real Secret Service shit."

"Don't bounce, Sean," Aldo said.

"Sorry."

"It's okay," Aldo said. "Go on." He put a lean, perfectly manicured hand on Sean's leg.

"Um," said Sean, "so, they let me in and I go into the living room and there's another dude in a black suit and he's standing by this Vietnamese man who's sitting on the couch with my mom. My mom stands up and says this is my dad and then my dad stands up and looks at me and he says in this thick accent that I have blue eyes. I don't say anything. He pats me on the head and pretty much goes. Never saw him again."

"Hmm," said Aldo. "I can never get over your eyes," Aldo said and leaned close to Sean. "I wish I could drink them."

Sean thought of laughing but no laughter would come. He thought of running but his legs wouldn't move.

"Hmm." Aldo stood and Sean could breathe again.

Aldo went over to the white dresser which and opened the top drawer. In the drawer were three black boxes. One of the boxes contained roughly a kilo of cocaine divided up into dime bags and 8-balls. The second box contained pot and pills packaged by weight, type and/or quantity. The third box had two 9 mms, fully loaded with the safeties off. "What can I do for you?" he said to Sean.

"Well, this party," Sean said. He knew what was in the boxes. "I'm hoping you could front me three more 8-balls and some X and maybe twenty dime bags of weed. I'll get the cash back to you tomorrow or tonight if you want."

"I would prefer tonight," Aldo said. He opened the first box and selected three Ziplocs that contained an equal amount of white powder in them. He placed these on the top of the dresser, next to the TV and then put the lid back on the box.

"No problem," Sean said.

"I'll be at Heaven," Aldo said and took the top off of the second box. He selected a blue pill bottle with 20 tablets in it and a large Ziploc that had twenty five little baggies with dried green herb in them. He placed these on the top of the dresser and then put the lid back on the box.

"There's a situation you might be able to help me with," he said and then he then took out a large plastic zip-lock bag from between two of the boxes and began putting all of the drugs in.

"What's the problem?" Sean said.

"Fucking VC," Aldo hissed.

"VC?"

"That's what they call themselves. Vietnamese kids. Came over here on boats as babies and now they're trying to take over my club," Aldo said. He left the now-full bag on the dresser and turned to look at Sean. "I have a plan, but, I need to be sure of you," he said. "How can I be sure of you when you owe me $1,565?"

"I thought it was, like $1000," Sean said. He was thinking that if he cut the three 8-balls down he could double his coke supply and make up a good portion of the debt if it was $1000 and with the sheet of acid to sell and all the pills he could probably get all the way to...

"One five six five," Aldo said.

"Yeah?"

"Yes."

Sean half-stood up and then sat back down. He'd probably have to borrow some from someone. "I paid you that $300 from the other night," he said.

"Yes, but you still haven't made good on what Leroy owed you, which you owe to me."

"Well, that's how I got the drums and stuff." Maybe Raven would lend him some, he thought.

"You said you were going to sell them."

"I sold the guitars."

"For how much?"

"$50."

"Where is it?"

"I spent it but…" Aldo closed his eyes. "Blow job?"

Aldo sighed, "I think not."

"Okay," Sean said. It hadn't been high on his to-do list today anyway. "You should come to the party tonight, Aldo. Hear us play."

Aldo glanced up at the ceiling, touched his left index finger to his tongue and then slid it over his left eyebrow. He clasped his hands behind his back and toed at the white carpet, the same kind as the one downstairs with the same fluffy snow texture.

"I don't really do parties," he said and moved toward Sean. He stood over him, so that he had to pin almost to his chest to talk.

"Do you still carry that knife?"

"Yeah," Sean said.

"May I see it?"

"Yeah," Sean said but he wanted to say, 'no'. He wanted to go to the dresser and slide all the drugs into his pouch and get out, because Aldo had that look on his face like he was about to do something he'd seen done in a movie. His skin felt tighter and his feet felt twitchy but he pulled the knife from his pocket and handed it to Aldo.

Aldo undid the clasp at the base and slowly folded down the two sides, revealing the long, thin blade. He ran his finger against it, testing its sharpness.

"You're good with all sorts of people," he said to Sean.

"I guess so."

"You are. Boys or girls."

"Yeah."

Aldo slid his tongue along the flat of the blade. "I don't want you to worry about the boys."

Sean's buttcheeks unclenched ever so much. "That's good."

Aldo wiped the knife across his leg. "Manny and I had a talk with one."

Sean had never been witness to one of Aldo's little talks but he'd heard they involved barrels, bullwhips and jell-o.

"Your hand, please," Aldo said.

"What?"

His eyes were as soft as a field of poppies. He held the blade in his right hand and extended his left, palm up, fingers slightly splayed, waiting. Sunlight filtered through the white venetian drapes.

"Please," he said.

"Aldo," Sean said, unconsciously putting his hands behind his back.

"I don't want to have to ask again," Aldo said.

Even in the cool air of the apartment, Sean began to sweat. He felt an icy drop roll down his spine. He gave Aldo his left hand, placed it as one would a duckling into the mouth of a crocodile. Aldo took Sean's hand and grasped it firmly at the wrist.

"Did you notice how when they first started coming to the club, the boys would sit the girls down and leave them there? Sometimes they would ask permission to dance so sometimes they got to dance. Did you notice that?"

"No," Sean said.

"I did. I notice things like that. I want you to talk to one of the girls."

Sean rolled and shook his head. "I don't speak Vietnamese."

94

"I've noticed some of them speak English. They must get very bored sitting in a corner, only able to dance with each other. I'm sure you'll find the one willing to stray."

Aldo smiled and it was like the benevolence of a Caesar falling upon Sean as rose petals might.

"Now, these VC have this ritual. They put a slice on the left hand." Aldo shook his head. "I don't know why they do it, but I need you to look like one of them. You already mostly look like one of them. You will need sunglasses to cover those arresting eyes of yours."

Sean tried to pull away, pull away and run, but Aldo held him fast.

"Now, now, hold still," he said as he drew the blade across Sean's palm.

The pain was like thunder. It came after the flash. It came as a surprise even as it was expected. Sean watched his skin part, saw bright red blood pump out but only after the momentary delay, only after the briefest of appreciative moments, when Sean thought his blood looked so pretty, did the pain rip at him, bend his knees and tighten his teeth.

He did not scream.

Kitten slithered up from Raven's lap. She turned with a wild smile. She was going to kiss Raven, lift up her shirt and play with her nipples, peel off her pants and give her a good going after. But just as her lips parted, and

Raven saw the flash of silver stabbed into an apple red tongue; Kitten saw a white van pass, like a whale along the side of the ship. Her eyes fixed on it, her breath caught in her chest and her arms began to shake. White vans carried straps and jackets.

Raven saw her friend's face freeze. She saw her gripping at the seat with clawed fingers. "What is it?" Raven said.

"Van," Kitten said.

Raven turned her head. The white van pulled into a driveway, paused, backed up and turned back towards them.

Kitten scrambled to the floorboards, tucking herself into a tiny ball. Raven slunk in her seat. Her right hand felt the hard metal of the butt of the gun. She watched as the white van passed them again. Behind the wheel was a plain looking man in a plain blue shirt, dark sunglasses and a plain black hat who did not look at them.

"If the bass is the heartbeat," Zac said, "what are the drums?"

Manny leaned forward. "Drums are the feet. They can run, walk or dance."

"What's the guitar?"

Manny leaned back and grabbed his crotch.

Zac snorted. "We have a girl guitarist."

"Sorry bro," Manny said.

"She's really good."

"Cool."

Zac wanted a cigarette but he didn't see an ashtray and didn't know if it was allowed. "Music is in the skin, yo." Manny slapped his arm. "I'm gonna make records, bro. Aldo's gonna set me up."

Zac tapped at the bass again. "What's the Jose Cruz thing?"

Manny's face went as hard as a face that fat can go.

"We don't talk about that shit."

Zac couldn't imagine what the former left fielder for the Houston Astros, the guy who, when he came to the plate, everyone would yell, 'CRUUUUUUUUZZZ' for as long as they could, would have to do with these guys but he now knew definitely not to bring it up again.

"What's the singer?" he said.

"Singer's the face." He lifted one side of his voluminous ass and farted, a long, glorious, gaseous release. "Or the soul," he said. "Depends on the singer. Good singer is both."

"We have to go. We have to go. We have to go," Kitten kept saying.

"We can't go," Raven said. "The guys aren't back yet."

"WE HAVE TO GO!" Kitten leapt up on the seat and clawed at Raven.

97

"Kitten! Calm down!"

Her claws became soothing strokes. "Please, Raven. Please." She darted her head to look out the window. The white van had parked a block down. The plain man had not gotten out. "They've come to get me."

"Kitten..."

Kitten faced Raven. Her face was drawn tight. Her eyes had gone hard and brittle as coal. "I won't go back."

"They're not."

"TAKE ME HOME!" Kitten flailed at Raven with her tiny fists.

Raven dropped her clove on the floorboard as she fought to defend herself. She managed to grab Kitten by both wrists and shove her back. Kitten hissed and bit, pulling Raven's arms toward her and sinking her teeth in. Raven screamed, wrenched her right arm free and punched Kitten in the side of the head and punched her again before she let go.

Kitten retreated to the far side of the car. Blood trickled from the piercings in her right eyebrow. Raven rubbed at the deep marks on her arm. Between them, a cauldron boiled. Raven could smell rubber burning.

"Please," Kitten wept. "Take me home."

Raven saw smoke rising from near her feet. She looked down and saw the clove smoldering on the floor mat, burning a black circle in the fuzzy rug. She picked it up and tossed it out the window.

"Please," Kitten said.

Raven bit her lip, rubbed her arm and turned the key in the ignition.

"Don't bleed on my carpet," Aldo said and released Sean's hand. Sean stood, wrapping his hand in his t-shirt, trying not to let a drop spill, tears from his blue eyes running down his brown cheeks. "Use the bathroom," Aldo said with a sigh.

Sean ran to the bathroom and put his hand under the tap. He turned it on cold and bore the pain by clamping his teeth together. The blood flowed freely, turning the drain a crimson swirl. He needed to wrap it in something but he didn't dare use one of the perfectly folded white towels and he was even worried about touching the toilet or tissue paper. Holding his hand over the sink as best he could, he pulled off his t-shirt and wrapped it around and around into a big green mitt. He held this to his chest. With his other hand he wiped the blood from the sink, moving the water around to wash it away. He wiped at his eyes and the snot coming from his nose with the back of his hand and tried to wash this too. When it all seemed like it was clean, he shut off the tap. He turned. Aldo was standing in the doorway holding the bag in one hand and the knife in the other.

Sean took a step back.

Aldo dropped the bag on the counter and then ran the knife under the sink. There was little blood on it but Aldo made certain that it was clean. He left it in the sink and then swiped a tissue from a box and wiped the blade. He dropped the tissue in the trash receptacle then folded the knife and replaced the clasp. He then dropped it back in Sean's pocket before turning and picking up the bag.

"Allow me," he said.

Aldo slid Sean's hip pack around, pulled it towards him, unzipped it, and stuffed the bag of drugs in. Sean watched, and waited and felt the throbbing of his hand. Aldo closed the pouch and stepped back. Sean felt the sweep of his gaze, from his hair to his eyes, down his naked torso to the t-shirt wrapped around his hand, his thin brown torso, red plaid pants and red Chucks. Aldo stared at the shoes and then he reached into his pocket and slid out a sheaf of bills folded into a silver clip. He extracted one of these bills, a $100 one, and put the rest back and then tucked the bill into the same pocket as the knife.

"Buy yourself some new shoes," he said and turned away. "And sunglasses," Aldo added. "You'll need to hide those Irish eyes." He went into his bedroom and shut the door, leaving Sean in a bathroom that wasn't his, on the second floor of an apartment he didn't want to be in anymore.

"See you tonight," Sean called and thudded down the steps to find Zac plucking out a steady beat while Manny tapped his fat fingers on the back of the sofa.

"Let's bowl," Sean said to Zac.

Zac stood and slung the bass behind him.

"Thanks, Manny," he said. "See you."

"No problem, bro," said Manny. "Peace."

Sean opened the door with his good hand and danced out. As Zac passed through and turned to close it he saw Manny lift the gun from the table and slide it between the couch cushions

After the deliciously cool air of the apartment, the mid-day heat hit Zac and Sean again like a hammer. They bowed their heads against its weight and stiffened their walks against its jelly-inducing hum.

"What happened to your shirt?" Zac said.

"Occupational hazard," Sean said.

Sean quickened his step and led Zac through the slithering paths of the apartment complex until they got to the gate. He lifted the latch and shouldered it open. Zac caught the gate as it swung back towards them and then followed Sean across the street and up the sidewalk.

After a minute they stopped. They looked around.

"This is where they were, right?" Zac said.

Sean twisted around. "Where the fuck's the car?"

Zac looked up the block and down the block. Sean looked down the block and up the block. In the space recently occupied by a large black '58 Buick Roadster, there now rested a teal Tercel with a Don't Mess With Texas bumper sticker.

101

"Is this the right spot?" Zac asked.

"I think so," said Sean. He stumbled down the block three cars, stood on his tiptoes, looked left and then right and into one of the houses because he thought he saw someone moving. Zac had gone up the other way and was pretty much doing the same thing. Neither one of them saw a big black '58 Buick Roadster.

"They left us!" said Sean. "They fucking left us!" He lifted his arms out and then placed them on top of his head, then suddenly became conscious of the blood soaked t-shirt on his left hand and his hip pouch belt sliding over his skin, and just how much shit he had in there. He quickly dropped his arms and inconspicuously tried to hold the pouch or hide it, hoping no one asked what was in it or about what happened to his hand, which hurt like fuck, and how was he going to play drums now or play their gig and get rich and famous?

"You stepped in some gum," Zac said.

"What?"

Zac pointed to Sean's left shoe. Sean looked down, lifted it and saw the sticky white strings rising from the sidewalk.

"Goddamn it," he said and scraped his shoe along the pavement, trying to rub the gum off. "God fucking damn it! God damn fucking gum!" he yelled. The scraping and rubbing wasn't working. Sean sat down and pried away at the gum with his fingers, holding his wrapped hand away.

Tears welled up and rolled down his face. He hated the entire world and all the gum-dropping, hand-slashing assholes in it.

"You all right, dude?"

Sean look up at Zac. He didn't say anything. He just looked up at him, all the way up and over him, into the blue cloudless sky. He stood up, scraped his shoe over the concrete one more time and said, "Fine."

Zac shifted his weight from one jump-booted foot to the other. "My sister's place isn't too far from here. Just over by the Menil," Zac said. "If she's home she might give us a ride to my place and then we can get my car."

"Okay," Sean said.

"Do you need to go to the hospital?"

"No," Sean said. "I just need a band-aid."

"My sister's roommate is a nurse."

"Cool," Sean sniffed his fingers. "Spearmint," he said.

"Spearmint gives me headaches. I like wintermint," Zac said.

"Which way?" Sean said, as he swiped dirt and debris from the seat of his pants and looked around. No cop cars were rolling down the street. No neighbors were out and about. A gray car was going into an apartment complex up the way and a guy was pulling a cake out of a white van but nothing else was happening except they were standing there like two idiots in the middle of the day, sweating and bleeding.

Zac nodded down the street. "That way," he said.

The two boys walked.

"I knew this girl," Sean said. "She orange tic-tacs. Just the orange ones. She would eat a whole box in, like, thirty seconds. Swear to God, I bought her a box on the way into this movie and she had eaten the whole thing by the time we sat down and I had to go back and get her a box of Skittles," he said and eyed the bottom of his shoe.

Zac laughed.

"Got a smoke?"

Zac dug into his pocket for his smokes. He pulled out two cigarettes, stuffed both in his mouth, lit them and handed one to Sean.

"Thanks," said Sean.

Sean drew in the smoke. It helped but he wanted one or two or ten of the painkillers in his bag. He didn't dare open it out here. When they got to Zac's sister's house he'd pop a pill and pack a bowl and all would be right in the universe.

"Goddamn, it's fucking hot," he said.

"My sister's roommate is hot," Zac said. "And her name's Delicious."

"Seriously?"

"Delicious Jackson."

"Fuck," Sean said. "Girls get all the cool names."

7.

The third thing Kitten told Raven after she had woken up in the hospital was that the doctors had said Raven had an eating disorder and that Raven's mother had said that was bullshit. When Raven asked Kitten what she was in for, Kitten showed her the bandages on her arms.

"I cut myself," she said. "A little bit too deep this time."

Two weeks into her employment at Nan's Record Store, Kitten and Raven had taken a break together. They kicked asphalt pebbles at the dumpster and then Raven heard the sizzle of flesh as Kitten introduced the burning end of her cigarette to her arm and watched her silver sparkled lips peel back from her teeth.

Kitten had peeled down her glove and Raven had seen the scores of thin white lines, like tally marks, always in threes, up and down the arm. These marks were polka-dotted by little melted craters.

"They used to bleed people to let the demons out," she had said. "Did you know that?"

"I think I read it somewhere," Raven said.

"It doesn't work. So now I'm trying to burn the fuckers." Kitten's smile stretched up to her ears and implied the doom of a mouse.

Raven had seen Kitten do the cigarette trick a few times since but never the razor and never this. She'd never seen Kitten shut down, curled up in the corner of her studio apartment, a dark purple sheet wrapped around her, her eyes open before the purple painted wall.

They'd had to pass the white van to escape the street where they left the boys, Kitten cowering on the floorboards, Raven glancing back. It took fifteen minutes to get to Kitten's place and she hadn't spoken the entire way. Raven tried talking to her, tried telling her there was no one following them but Kitten just shook her head. When they got to the dilapidated apartment complex with its greenish-bluish-yellowish-waterish filled pool, Raven parked the car and pried her out. Under the twisted branches of a pecan tree infested with grackles keeping up a continuous chorus of what sounded like old time cash registers ringing up sales, Kitten walked bent over like a woman about to give birth. Raven helped her up the steps to her door, took the keys from her bag, opened the door and guided her in. Kitten sprung from Raven's grasp and dashed to the corner of her room, dragging the sheet off the bed along the way and bundling herself up.

107

Raven tried talking to her some more, tried petting her and brushing back her hair but Kitten wouldn't move. She wouldn't talk and she wouldn't close her eyes.

Finally, Raven went to pee. The bathroom was purple. Purple towels lay in stank piles on a purple rug. A chaos of purple candles, orange pill bottles, white and green and red sprays, pastes and bath salts crowded the top of the toilet and the edges of the sink. The medicine cabinet hung loose and Raven glanced in. It was the same as the last time she'd seen it, stuffed full of lipsticks, mascaras, eyeliners, Q-tips and Strawberry Shortcake band-aids. Raven closed the little door. The mirror was cracked and splintered, it reflected her face in shards and chunks. She turned on the cold tap.

Raven borrowed some of Kitten's face cleanser and scrubbed off the grime of the morning. She washed out a little purple glass and took a drink. She found a dryish towel in the pile of clothes and such that had been dumped in the small bathroom closet under the shelves sparsely populated by toilet tissue and anti-fungal cleaning products. She toweled her face dry. She caught herself looking at herself in the mirror. Her eye sockets had sunk into her skull. The skin seemed translucent at her cheekbones and along her jaw. She pressed her face into the towel again then dropped it on the floor as she left.

Kitten was still in the corner, half-buried under another pile of clothes. Everything else was all over the place. There was a small bookcase crowded with knick-knacks, ashtrays, a whip, and two stuffed animals, a kitten and a bear. A boom box sat in a nest of tapes and CD's. There were stacks of books against the walls; French erotica, German existentialism, Russian realism, American beats and South American poetry. The kitchen counter was covered in incense burners and unopened mail. The sink was full of scabbed-over dishes. There were two gallon jugs of red wine against the wall. One was about half-empty. Reflected light made a purple and white halo on the purple wall. Raven sat down on the full-sized bed that flopped on the floor without a frame and pulled her bag up with her.

She dug out some foundation and spread it across her face, starting at her sunken eyes and moving outward, up and down. When this was done she could look at herself again and pulled out the eye-liner to circle her gray tinted whites with inky black. She decided to draw a leaf tasseled swirl down from her right eye and an ankh from the left. She replaced the eye-liner with lipstick and colored in her pale pink lips white. When she was done she snapped the compact shut and chunked it back into her bag.

"Kitten?" she said.

"I'm in my dark and furry place," a child's voice whispered.

"Coming out anytime soon?"

Nothing.

109

Raven lay back on the bed. A purple tie-dyed sheet had been pinned to the ceiling. The shapes made a vortex that might shoot her up into the sky. If Kitten were a song, Raven thought, it would take ten days to play, would include eighteen hours of silence, three counts of arson and in the end only a handful of audience members would survive.

"She's home," Zac said. He stepped up the little walk to the front porch of a fat gray stucco house with heavy black iron bars on the windows and doors. "Car's here," he said.

The car was a little red Storm with a long blue scrape along the passenger side door. It waited next to the house in the driveway behind a tin colored Toyota two-door.

Zac rang the doorbell while Sean tapped his feet on the steps. They hadn't seen a cop car the whole walk but Sean had never stopped looking around. Along the way he'd discovered that the more Sean urged Zac to speed up, the slower he went. Sean would skip ahead and then have to pause, like waiting for an old dog that measured its progress by sniffs and scents rather than blocks or districts. When Zac caught up, he apologized for being slow but that hadn't made him move any quicker. Sean had almost started screaming but he couldn't afford attention, so he did his best to move Zac along while wincing from the pain and adjusting his hip pouch as it slid around from all the weight inside. Finally, he ducked into a hedge

110

and dug out a Vicodin. It was just now kicking in nicely. Someone had turned down the oven called Houston. The leaves of the live oaks were green and the birds sang a lovely song.

The interior door opened. Zac was greeted by an avalanche of dark cleavage held back by a white halter top. Attached to the cleavage was a young woman with a wide smile, her frizzed out hair pulled back tight by a blue band that matched her jogging shorts. She wasn't wearing shoes.

"Hi, Zac," she said with a wide-eyed smile.

"Hi, Del," Zac said.

"Is that Kyle?" a voice cracked from somewhere inside.

Del turned her head. Zac's eyes traced the curve of her breasts and down the rest of her to her thighs. "It's your brother!" Del said, opened the iron gate and stood aside.

"Thanks," Zac said and went inside. "This is Sean," he said and waved behind him to the boy who was now stumbling to the door.

"Hi," he said. "I'm Sean."

"I'm Delicious," Del said.

"I'm barely palatable, myself," Sean said, tripping through the door.

Del laughed. "That's almost a new one!" Her teeth were as white as icing and as clean as hotel sheets. Sean watched as she closed the gate and the door.

111

"Would you mind if I fall madly, deeply in love with you?" he said.

"Not at all," she said.

"What's with the guitar?" the other voice snapped and Sean turned to see a tall girl in another white halter top with denim cut-offs come into the front room from a dark hall. While this girl did not occupy the same volume of halter top, her shorts capped long legs that Sean would gleefully attempt to climb, with or without a harness.

"It's my bass," Zac said to his sister.

His sister put one hand on one hip and cocked it out at a sharp angle. "What's with the bass then, Zac?"

They said each other's names the way brothers and sisters do, with every grievance, every kidnapped decapitated dream doll or back yard buried Matchbox racing car embodied.

"I'm in a band," Zac said.

"Since when?"

"Since this morning." Zac leaned the bass against a speckled blue sofa. "We're playing a party tonight," he said. "You and Del should come."

"Seriously," Sean said, sliding closer to Del. "Y'all should definitely come."

Del shot a quick glance at Zac's sister.

"Maybe," she said. She looked back at Sean. "Why is your hand all wrapped up?"

"Nothing." he said. "Fell down on the sidewalk."

"How can you fall on a sidewalk?" Zac's sister shifted herself to her other hip.

"Tripped on some gum," Sean said. He turned to Del's breasts and then looked up to find her face patiently waiting for him. "Zac says you're a nurse."

Del's eyebrows raised and lowered, her lips curled in and then pouted out. "Almost. One more semester, but I can fix you up."

"You better," Zac said. He schlumped onto the couch. "He's the drummer."

The edges of Lori's lips turned down in the coldest meanest way, just the way her mother sometimes did as Del led Sean past Lori and down the hall. The walls were bare and painted a sort of beige, but it was hard to tell as the curtains had been drawn against the afternoon sun and the hallway was cool and dark. Del led Sean past a bedroom where he noticed a neatly made pink-sheeted bed with four or five stuffed bears on it.

"That's my room," Del said.

"Look's delicious," said Sean.

"Oh," Del sighed, "silly boy."

She pointed him into the bathroom.

113

"What's going on, Zac?" Lori said.

"Can you give us a ride back to my place?" Zac said and crossed one leg over the other so that the ankle of his boot rested on the other knee.

Lori sat down on the table in front of Zac. He watched her sit and then looked down at his boot and started twisting one of the laces.

"What's going on?" Lori leaned forward and put her hand on the toe of his boot. He hated seeing her all folded up like that and how her boobs would push up together and how he would accidently have to see them do that.

"We just got stranded over here and need a ride back to my place."

"How did you get stranded?"

Zac moved his foot away. "Some miscommunication with the rest of the band," Zac said. He looked around the apartment. Boxes were stacked against the wall by the door. There was writing on the boxes. LORI'S BOOKS one said and LORI'S KITCHEN on another.

"Moving again?"

Lori looked over at the boxes and back to her brother.

"I'm moving in with Kyle," she said.

"Don't do it," Zac said. "Kyle's a dick." He let go of the lace.

"He is not."

"He is." Zac said.

"He was an officer in Operation Desert Storm."

114

"Still a dick."

"You're just very difficult to get along with these days," she said.

"It's always difficult to get along with a dick." Zac picked up the lace again.

"Well," Lori said and stood up. "I hope you'll try a little harder to get along with him because I love him."

Zac shook his head and ground his teeth. He wanted a cigarette but Lori didn't let him smoke in the apartment. He was always wanting cigarettes these days. He smoked packs and packs. He woke up and had a smoke. He had a smoke with his coffee and his morning dump. He smoked on his way to school and on the way to class. After class, he had a smoke. He smoked after lunch and while he did his homework. He smoked while he played video games and before bed he had one last one. Each one was like his first one. Each time he saw the blue tinted smoke rising and curling and fading away he saw the blood-sodden floor of the house down in Kemah and six bare feet all tangled up.

"Do you want some water?" Lori said.

"Take a beer." He looked up hopefully.

"You're not 21."

"So?" Zac hunched forward.

Lori shrugged. "Help yourself," she said and stepped out of the way.

Zac stood and went into the kitchen. Lori followed him. He opened the fridge. Half of the shelves were filled with the various items one would expect to find in a fridge occupied by two physically fit females. There was juice and soy milk and Tupperware containers with leftovers. Carrots, celery, and lettuce were stuffed into the produce compartment. Yogurts and dressings occupied another shelf along with a container of hummus and another of tofu. The other half was nearly empty except some bread and cheese and four Shiners. Zac took one of the Shiners and closed the door. He slid over to a drawer and opened it to find towels.

"Next one," said Lori.

Zac opened the next one and took out a can opener with a beer key on one end. He pried off the cap and took a long swig, watching sunlight dissipate and deffuse in the brown glass of the bottle.

"I have dad's check for you," Lori said.

"Thanks," Zac said and took another long drink. He felt the coolness enter him, flowing down and then circulating throughout his bloodstream.

"He got another offer on the beach house," she said.

"And…?"

Lori leaned against the counter and then hoisted herself up on it. "We'll see," she said. She looked down at her nails and picked at a cuticle. Zac leaned against the counter next to the fridge.

116

"I've been calling you for three days," Lori said.

"You could have just stopped by."

"That place is gross." Lori hopped down, took two steps forward, reached out, took the beer from him and took a drink. "Ugh," she said and made a yuk face. "Tastes like cigarettes," she said.

"How can you even tell?"

Lori thrust the beer back at him. "You need to quit."

"I just started," Zac said. He took another drink. He couldn't taste cigarettes. "How is dad?" he said.

"He's having more tests."

"How's mom?"

"You should go see her," Lori said.

"I will," Zac said. "I need to do laundry anyway."

Lori shook her head the same way she'd been shaking her head since she was three.

"We've all had a hard time, Zac."

"I know."

She put her hand to her forehead and brushed back a strand of hair. Lori was the sort of pretty it took a moment to recognize. She was too tall and not everything lined up at first. Her eyes seemed a shade too high and her chin a touch too low but when considered, when given a second glance, she was pretty in her way which was prettier than most. But there were brown boxes, no notes on the fridge, or pictures on the walls. Lori was always moving in or out, Zac thought. She was always moving on and hardly leaving any trace behind.

"It's okay to fall apart for awhile," Zac said.

"Is that right?"

"Give it a try," Zac said and drained the beer.

Lori folded her arms across her chest. "Then who would go get your check from dad?"

"I'd get it."

"Who would get dad to the hospital for his tests? Who would get Mom away from her office every once in awhile? Who would do all that?"

"We'd get by," Zac said. He put the beer down and went to his sister. He put his hands on her shoulders and looked deep into her eyes. "Fall apart," he said. "Do whatever you want."

"I'm in law school."

"Take a semester off. Go crazy. Run away. Send me postcards from Finland telling me you just stood naked under a waterfall and had a wild Viking orgy. But don't move in with Kyle."

"I love him," she said.

"You don't," he said. "You just miss James."

A fluffy cloud shaped like a turtle crawled across the sun and Lori's face reduced in hue.

His sister needed a hug and so Zac hugged her. They held onto each other against the tide of an entire world because only they knew what they missed and only they really cared. Other people missed other things and held on to other people but this was theirs. Lori sobbed and convulsed. Zac tried to remember the little things. He tried to remember the fort James and his dad had built in the backyard. He tried to remember the first time James let him play D&D with his teen-age friends. But all he saw, over and over, was the last light of the day on the bodies lying naked and twisted like bed sheets. He wanted to feel his big sister helping him up onto his bike again but all he could remember was the squishy, soaking rug under his feet. He wanted to hear her say she loved him and everything would be okay again but all he heard was the ocean outside the window, the waves rolling in and drawing out, the gulls calling and his own blood pulsing in his ears, mocking what had been splattered on the walls.

As they held each other, a key turned in the gate, the gate opened and then the front door. A man wearing khaki shorts, a blue polo and worn brown boat shoes entered the house.

"Hey," the man said, "what's going on?"

Lori pulled herself back and wiped at her eyes.

"Kyle," she said. She continued to hold Zac around the waist with one arm while continuing to wipe her face with the other. "Just a sister/brother moment."

"You okay?" Kyle said. He spun his car keys on his finger.

"Yeah," Lori said, releasing Zac and stretching her arms and herself towards Kyle, moving to him and wrapping her arms around him. She bent her head down and kissed him.

"Hey," she said, pulling back from Kyle, "Zac's in a band."

"That right?" Kyle said. He held Lori with one arm, still spinning the keys.

"Yeah," Zac said. "We're playing a party tonight. Y'all should come."

"We should," Lori said.

"What's your band's name?" Kyle said.

"Double Murder Suicide," Zac said.

"What THE FUCK!" Lori screamed.

As Sean sat on the lid of the toilet and Del knelt before him, cleaning, patting, bandaging and wrapping his hand, Sean did kick flips across her sleek, pulled back hair. He did a shimmy across her lips, so wide and full to the lovely little song they hummed as she worked. He went full stage dive into her cleavage, so proudly displayed, so artfully constructed. These fantasies occupied Sean as Del snipped off the end of the bandage and taped it up.

"All done," she said, looking, up at him, smiling.

120

"Thank you," he said. He tested the flex of the bandage, felt it crinkle and bend. It would do, it would definitely do. He pulled his pouch around. "Do you want some pot or anything?"

"No thanks," she said.

She put her hands on his knees and pressed herself up, her chest rising in front of him like a pair of hot air balloons. Electricity shot straight up from his balls. He would grab her and take her, kiss her and mount her. He would compose sonnets for her and bring her flowers. He would row her down a gently drifting stream, place strawberries between her teeth and make love to her as they dropped over a three hundred foot waterfall. He would make her bark like a harbor seal. If there was ever anything in this world that Sean wanted to do it was Delicious.

Then he heard the shouting.

"HOW THE FUCK COULD YOU GIVE A BAND A NAME LIKE THAT!"

"Seriously, dude," Kyle added. "With all your sister's been through…"

"Shut up, Kyle," Zac said.

"Hey…"

"We have to own this," Zac said, "or it will own us forever."

"That's what I said," said Sean.

121

Lori and Kyle turned to look at Sean. His hand had been neatly wrapped in white gauze and medical tape, he held his hip pouch by the strap and there was the distinct outline of a boner at the crotch of his lime green pants.

"Who the fuck are you?" said Kyle.

"Who the fuck are you?"

"I'm Kyle."

"I'm Sean."

The dark brown hardwood floors, the bare walls, the boxes in their stacks. Del edged into the room.

Lori looked directly at Zac and said, "It's disrespectful to James."

"His first band was called Crack Baby Sunshine," Zac said. "I'm pretty sure he'd be cool with it."

"What do you think Mom would say?" Lori said.

"Mom's in a coma," said Zac. "And dad's in a bottle. Maybe it will wake them up."

"It's really just, really disrespectful, Zac."

Zac pounded towards Kyle. "SHUT UP, KYLE!"

Kyle took a step back and then stood his ground. "I know thirteen ways to break every bone in your body."

"That's just stupid."

Kyle and Zac and Lori and Del all turned to look at Sean.

"I mean," Sean said, "there's like, what, a thousand bones in the human body? And if you knew thirteen ways to break every one that would be like, what, 130,000 different variations. I'm just saying I seriously doubt it." Sean shook his head knowingly.

Zac's desire to smash and thrash did not fully abate but it eased enough for him swallow the spit that had pooled in corners of his mouth.

He paused to measure his pain against the weight of the world. It was a constant shimmer before his eyes. It clouded and colored every sight. When he looked at his sister, he had to look through a stained glass window.

Zac went to the bass and grabbed it by the neck. "Just give me my check and we'll go."

"I won't get it for you anymore," she said.

"FINE!" Rage was easy. Yell and stomp and scream, smash trashcans and curse trees in the middle of the night, and everyone will leave you alone.

Lori left Kyle's side and stalked down the hallway to her bedroom, passing Del along the way. Zac moved toward the door. Sean looked around.

"We still need a ride, dude?" Sean said.

"No prob," Del said.

Del scooped a set of keys out of a bowl on a small table by the door. She slipped on some flip-flops as Lori returned from the hall and held out a folded check to her brother. Zac took it and stuffed it in the back pocket of his shorts.

"Zac, I just…"

"Let's go," Zac said and stomped out the door. A silver Ford F-150 King Cab now sat behind the little red Storm which was parked behind the tin colored Toyota. "Somebody's going to have to move some cars," he said and pulled out a cigarette.

8.

Raven stood in a wide green meadow dotted with Black Eyed Susans and Bluebonnets. She wore a thin Cleopatra style dress, the color and the weight of the clouds that smeared across the sky. Sparrows swooped about, singing their songs and gossiping about bugs. Bees darted between her legs. Her belly grew as she walked. At the crest of a hill, beneath a pecan tree, she stopped and looked down. She felt with her hands the skin stretched out and within she felt a thing turning and twisting. The sun glowed and gave the green leaves a golden aura. She would squat there, beneath the tree and deliver unto the world a child of light. She felt a tender kick. She cooed and stroked her belly, but the belly turned black.

She felt the thing coil within her and then strike. A rib cracked, and even as she cried out in agony, she felt the thing coil again. A black claw erupted from her womb. Black blood sprayed from her, and where it fell, the flowers turned to ash. The sun was swallowed by a spreading gloom, and thunder boomed from the distant mountains, and with each percussion, the thing within her ripped another seam until it was able to crawl out.

It was hideous, a black feathered human face attached to a crow's body. The slimy, flapping spawn groped for her breast. Its black tongue slithered out and over fanged teeth, and slimed over her engorged breasts, which were full of tar. The thing clamped onto a nipple, dug its teeth in and began to suck the very essence of her soul.

"Ow!" Raven squawked and opened her eyes to find Kitten staring at her. Raven's nipples stung. There was a knocking at the door.

"You okay?" Kitten said.

Raven rubbed her chest. "What happened?"

"You were having a nightmare. You were screaming," Kitten said. "I twisted your nipples to wake you up."

"Kitten!" Sean called from the door.

"Couldn't you have just shook me or something," Raven said.

"Listen," Kitten shot a glance at the door and then shoved her face back at Raven. "That night of the Cure concert some crazy shit happened and I ended up in County Psych for six months. They came for me in a white van."

"Oh," Raven said.

"So, I'm sorry I lost it." Kitten hopped off of Raven.

"Are you okay?" Raven rose to her elbows.

Kitten peeked through the peep hole. "Fucking peaches." She opened the door.

"What the fuck?" Sean said, standing in his own sweat.

"Fuck you," Kitten replied.

Sean entered, followed by Zac and his bass. Raven sat up.

"Okay," Sean said and then stood there nodding his head. Zac looked down at Kitten who looked up at him. They both raised their eyebrows and looked away. Raven bit her lip. "Are we going to do this thing or what?"

"What thing?" Kitten said.

Sean looked at her. "This band thing!"

"What happened to your hand?" Raven said.

Sean turned to her. "Long story. Actually, not a long story but I don't want to go into it. What happened to you two?"

"Long story," Kitten said and folded her arms across her chest.

"You like purple," Zac said.

"Yes," she said.

"Purple's nice."

"It's like a three day bruise."

They all said nothing for a minute. Zac turned his head from here to there, snatching glimpses of Kitten and scanning to find a pattern to all that purple. She liked purple, Zac concluded, but she only liked it here, in her apartment. His guess was, she never took purple outside.

The pain in Raven's nipples receded but the dream was still at the periphery of her mind. The less she ate, the more she dreamed, dreams more vivid and violent. If she took her happy-mood pills her dreams were drab and dull but so was her playing.

Sean looked at Zac and then at Kitten and then at Raven.

"Are we going to do this thing?"

"I want to," said Raven.

"Me too," said Zac.

"Kitten?"

"Fine," she said.

"Good." Sean looked at his watch. "Shit. Kitten, do you have any baking soda?"

"There might be a box in the fridge that's been in there for twenty years or something," she said.

"Excellente," Sean said and bounced into the kitchen. Zac moved out of the way and with nowhere else to go, he chanced a weak smile to Raven and sat on the edge of the bed. Sean opened the fridge, quickly found the box of baking soda among the sparse contents and took it out. He had to balance it on the edge of the fridge until he could shove the pans and glasses, mail and mustard-covered plates into a dusty corner. He took the baking soda down and set it on the counter then opened his pouch.

Zac rested the bass against the pile of clothes. He mumbled something in the vague direction of Raven.

"What?" she said.

"I've been practicing," he said.

"That's good," she said. Raven stuffed a purple covered pillow in the uncomfortable gap between her back and the wall. She pulled her long white hair around and started teasing out any clumps with her nails. Kitten came over and sat between them. She watched Raven and then looked over at Zac. She got up on her knees and pulled two chunks of his hair up.

"We should spike up your hair," she said. She let the hair flop back down, settled back and tapped on his hand. "We should do your nails too."

Zac looked up at her and then down at his hands. For a man his size, they were not excessively large hands. There was a dull white circle just above the first knuckle of his left middle finger where a wart had been removed when he was ten. There was a faint scar on the right pinkie where he cut himself playing with James' pocket knife, and a bluish dot on the pad of his left palm from where he had dropped a pencil he was fiddling with at lunch, his Senior year, and instinctively dropped his hand to retrieve it, only to feel a sharp pain as the pencil had landed eraser down, point up, his reach for it too quick. He raised his hand to eye level and found the pencil impaled in his skin. He pulled the pencil out to discover a tattooed graphite dot that would remain with him for all his days, so tiny he would never have to explain it unless he wanted to. It was his secret tattoo. He looked at the dirt encrusted nails.

"Okay," he said.

Kitten shoved herself from the wall and directed herself towards her bag. "Raven, there's a bottle of Elmers somewhere over near that little table over there or it might be in the bathroom."

Raven surveyed the pile of crap she had been directed to investigate. She thought she saw something move. "We should use Knox," she said.

Kitten snatched up the bag and went to the bed. "No time and I don't have any."

Raven rolled towards the corner as Sean poured a roughly measured mixture of cocaine and baking soda into a not disgusting bowl he had found in a spider-web invaded cupboard while reserving a small pile of the coke on an untainted plate.

"So this is my plan," Sean said, wiping off a spoon and twisting it into the bowl.

Kitten dropped down to open the bag and dug past her pack of Marlboro Lights, past a mix-tape from some boy whose name she couldn't remember, and below some other shit before she pulled out a bottle of black nail polish. She spun around on her knees then crawled up onto the foot of the bed, next to Zac.

"Hand please," she said with a coquettish smile. Zac turned to her and placed his hand large, grimy hand in her silky covered one.

Raven found the glue under a funky smelling pair of panties and a Star Pizza box. She dropped it next to Zac. "Hairbrush?"

"Use the black one under the sink. Blow dryer is under there too."

Raven pressed herself up from the bed and went into the bathroom. Kitten twisted open the nail polish. Sean mixed and folded the two white powders together, enjoying the tingling dust that drifted and swirled about him. "We do this gig tonight...I mean, this is just the start," he said.

Kitten took Zac's right hand and placed it on her thigh just at the point where the dark tartan skirt stopped and her black tights took over. Her leg felt warm in Zac's hand and the drizzle of hairspray drops falling on his skin made him think of a light spring rain. Raven returned, plugged in the blow dryer in the outlet next to the bed, set it to the side, took up the brush and Zac's floundering hair as Kitten painted his index finger and then moved to the middle one, dipping and painting in a practiced rhythm. She leaned forward, concentrating and Zac felt her breath tickle the tiny hairs near the scar as Raven stretched his hair up and applied a thick glop of glue.

Sean paused in his slicing and dicing, stirring and sifting to look over his shoulder. "Y'all look like that scene in *Beauty and the Beast* where

131

the teacup and the dresser do up the Beast for dinner. Have you seen that movie? We should rent it and watch it on acid. It's a trip. Well, everything's a trip on acid." He turned back to his mixing. "That's why they call it a trip. Duh." The white powder mixed with white powder to make white powder. "So, there's an old factory just down the street from Steele's that these guys are converting to music studios and we should totally get one and practice all the time. I know this guy, Sharkey, he's got a four-track we can borrow to make a demo and then when we've got enough stuff we'll make a CD. We should find an old school bus to tour in, but, I don't know. We don't really need it. Everything fits in Raven's car."

Raven kept stringing out lengths of Zac's hair, moving his head this way and that, brushing in the glue and then hitting it with the dryer as Kitten did the ring finger and then the pinkie, delicately brushing the wet black paint across Zac's uneven nails. He felt hot and bothered, confined and constricted. His fingers couldn't breathe and his scalp was scorched but if ten years of Texas football had taught him anything it was to endure suffering without complaint.

Sean hooked a bump of the mix onto the nail of his pinkie and raised it to his nostril. He closed the other with a finger and took a snort. The pure stuff, the good stuff, was a sharp blast of heat that instantly transposed to an icy numbness combined with accelerated synapse response and a pronounced increase in one's opinion of oneself, in direct proportion

132

to the idiocy of the world surrounding. When cut too much with various household products, Sean found that the burning blast lingered, but the feeling of being a master of the known universe and beyond never reached full maturity. Sean, feeling the icy numb coming on, if a tad late, and feeling himself coming into his own as a musical pioneer and soon-to-be punk rock icon, judged the mix suitable and took up one of the emptied baggies to refill. "You don't have a scale do you, Kitten?"

"Sorry," Kitten said moving Zac's hand so she could get to the thumb. His fingers now touched the rounded side of her leg. He shifted his weight slightly and Raven's body leaned against him before she could re-balance herself. The process was not without some pleasure, and being the center of feminine attentions after so many months alone in dark rooms with Joy Division droning in the background was not entirely unwelcome.

Sean looked at the dusty baggie in his hand and the two on the counter. "Oh, well," he said. "Rough estimates," and began to fill the bags.

Kitten finished Zac's thumb and let go of his hand. Holding the brush out to the side, she reached for his left hand and Zac gave it to her. She placed it on her thigh, dipped the brush in the bottle and started with the thumb this time. Raven got off the bed, climbed over the pile of clothes and the bass and stood at his side, her sharp hips peeking out from her baggy

133

pants, regarding the lopsided crest. She bit her lip, released it and picked up the glue and brush again.

"So," Sean said, "we practice and we play around town and we record a demo and then a CD and we go on road trips. We do a couple of festivals and then we get signed by some indie label and we start doing the big bus tours and Lollapalooza and head over to Europe and Japan then...," Sean filled up two baggies with three spoonfuls a piece and was trying to judge how many spoonfuls equated an 8-ball. He had a wad of little baggies in his pouch and would cut the remainder into them, a spoonful a piece and sell them for $25. He found a little red Betty Boop spoon that would do the trick.

The air was thick with the intoxicating aromas of hot glue and nail polish. Zac's eyes glistened and his nostrils twitched. He felt encased. Kitten moved the thumb and slid Zac's hand around so she could get to the fingers. She started with the pinkie and as she leaned forward Zac felt her breath on his skin again while Raven's fingers played along his scalp.

"So we'll all be rich and move to LA and live in big fucking mansions," Sean went on, finishing Steele's 8-balls, digging out the dime bags and starting on them, "because we made our big sell-out album that our hard core fans hate but the masses just eat up and we end up opening up for U2 during their summer tour and then we get even bigger than U2 and they have to open for us, and we sold one of our tunes for a Super Bowl commercial and then, you know, the drugs start to catch up to me and I have to go into rehab."

He worked quickly, with practiced hands and chemical accelerant, buzzing on the odors trapped in the small room, popping open a baggie, sliding in a spoonful of coke, sealing it up and moving on to the next.

"Kitten's marriage to Johnny Depp falls apart. Raven's solo album, while critically acclaimed, is a commercial flop and Zac disappears after dabbling briefly in the porn industry. It turns out he moved to Maine and coaches junior high football. Kitten writes a memoir and Raven is missing and presumed dead. I've gone into movie producing."

As Sean sealed the last baggie and licked the spoon, Raven cut the power to the blow dryer and stood back.

"Rockin," she said.

Kitten leaned back and admired Raven's work. She said he looked real horror show and ducked her head back down to polish Zac's last littlest finger. She sat back up, pulled his hand to her mouth, looked up at him with her golden-showered green eyes and blew on each nail, one by one by one.

"Go take a look," she said.

Zac clambered off the bed. Standing, the little room felt much smaller. It took two small strides and he was in front of the cracked mirror. The Mohawk that he could never manage to get to stick up no matter how many packets of gelatin he smeared into it now stood proud, shiny and blue.

The fingers that had held a blade hours ago now popped out against his skin. Raven leaned against to door.

"Looks good," he said to her.

Kitten put the nail polish back in her bag and pulled out a smoke. She worried for a moment that the flame might ignite the fumes wafting about them but decided to chance it. Meanwhile, Sean pulled out a video rental card from his pouch and began chopping up the untouched small pile of coke on the plate into four long lines. This done, he brought the plate to the bed, set it down on the purple sheet and knelt before it. He pulled Aldo's $100 from his pouch rolled it into a straw and drew it along the first line, sucking up the icy heat with first one nostril and then the other.

As he arose he tilted his head back and breathed deeply in. He shook his head, his long dark hair twisting about and then his whole body shivered. He let out a yelp and proffered the straw to Kitten who rose up, found a tea stained cup to balance her cigarette on, then turned, took the straw and knelt beside Sean to the plate and the second line. She sucked up the line in four equal bursts, shivered, shook, giggled and snorted as Raven and Zac came back into the room. She held the straw aloft as she rubbed at her nose and dabbed at her tear filling eyes.

Sean edged over to the wall to make room for Raven, who took the straw in her long fingers, went to her knees and sucked up the third line.

When she was done, Raven arched back, just as Sean had. She pinched her nose with one hand and held the other out into the purple tinted air. Her eyes watered but she felt her stomach quiet and the rush filter through her. Sean took the $100 straw from her hand and offered with red rimmed eyes up to Zac.

"I've never done coke before," Zac said.

"Bust that cherry!" Sean cheered.

"It's good shit," Kitten choked out, sliding to the far wall, looking for her cigarette.

"Go on," Raven said, pinching and sniffing at her nose. She crawled backwards to make room.

Zac took the straw from Sean in his newly painted fingers, knelt onto his knees, leaned forward and snorted deep.

9.

The echoes of industrial fired metal amplified noise had subsided after the two hours of rehearsal, discovery, deviation and devastation conducted by Double Murder Suicide. Sitting in the middle of the wrestling ring, three of the four individuals that comprised the band saw the sun setting as the vast blue that blanketed the city all day shifted to a soft orange. The fourth band member picked at a string that had come loose from the seam of her satin gloves and watched Sean drip a line of super-glue into the cut on his hand..

Sean pressed the skin together, his face wincing. Del's bandaging had been beautiful and lasted about twenty minutes. His drums were spotted with blood but, by his estimation, two of the five songs they'd developed would become part of the seminal history of the band. Song number two featured Raven at her cataclysmic best, a burning, blasting nuclear bomb of a song with a churning, driving beat that he and Zac only fucked up a few times. The third song would also resound through the ages. A dynamic change from the second song, it was atmospheric, minimalistic, haunting and transitional. The first song was a short, straightforward thing, like a grocery cart on a downhill run, and the fourth song was a mess whose existence must surely be terminated if there were not the need for a fourth song. Hopefully, the crowd would forget about the fourth song after rocking out to the finale, DMS's adaptation of *Green Eggs and Ham* which should prove to be short, fast and highly moshable. It was, as yet, the only song with a title, and the only song with any lyrics or a person singing them.

This was the focus of the first official 'band meeting'. It was held in the center of Steele's wrestling ring. They sat cross-legged in a diamond aligned with the four posts of the ring, an ashtray that had been sculpted into the form of a hissing, fanged turtle at their center. It was an ancient configuration, one that made Zac think of Druids and Raven of medicine men.

"People are going to start showing up soon," Sean said. He was hunched forward, holding a cigarette and picking at the frayed and bloodied bandage on his hand.

"I know," Kitten said. Sitting opposite Sean, she held her own cigarette before her, her knees pulled up to her chest, and her head resting on those knees. She clicked the barbell in her tongue against her teeth.

"I can come up with something," Zac said. He rested with his arms behind him and then leaned forward, tapping an ash into the screaming turtle. "If you don't want to do it."

"I do want to do it," Kitten said as the smoke lingered in her vision.

139

"What's wrong?" Raven sat cross-legged with her elbows resting on her knees, her head craned forward. She resembled a scaffold draped in black cloth.

"There's nothing wrong," Kitten said, clicking away at her teeth. "I'm just not ready." She took a long drag of her cigarette. "I thought I was ready."

Raven leaned even farther forward, bit at her lip, extended a limb and touched Kitten's bare shoulder with her long, white fingers. "What can we do to help you get ready?"

Kitten dropped her head between her knees. The coke had worn off some time ago and she really didn't feel like doing any more at the moment. It made her feel thin and Raven was doing enough thin for all of them. She had listened to the three of them playing, scribbling in her notebook nothing but swirls and jagged lines. Sometimes she constructed an entire square.

"Words are hard," Kitten said. She shook off Raven's cold touch and stood. "You can't just play them."

"Where are you going?" Sean said.

"Out," she said.

"We need to rehearse this shit!" He sat up, his head turning as he followed Kitten, as she slid under the ropes and out of the ring. "Get back here!"

Kitten turned, her gloved hands balled into little fists. "Leave me alone!" she said and stomped her foot. "Jani ma!"

She kicked at the folding chair Steele used to practice shots to the head with and crumpled it with a crash. She stomped out the back door and into the back yard where she was met with a chorus of excited yelping and barking.

Zac, Sean and Raven watched her go. "Jani ma!" they heard her say and then the door slammed shut as such doors are wont to do.

Sean turned around. "Johnny Ma? What does that mean?"

"It's French," Raven said. "It basically means, 'That's enough,' but in a bigger way, sort of."

"I can come up with something," Zac said.

Sean looked down at him. "Can you sing and play at the same time?"

"I can barely play anyway so what does it matter?" Zac shrugged.

"Fuuuuuuck," Sean sighed.

"You're getting better," Raven said to Zac with a smile that was almost like a human smile.

"Thanks," Zac said.

"You've just got to let go."

"I know," he said. In the past two hours he'd managed to sync' up to Sean's eclectic beats for the most part and hit his changes. He'd come up with a cool intro for that first song but the thing he hadn't been able to do, the thing that was missing and he knew it, was the thing they used to do when he played with James; which was to play with wild abandon, to just not give a fuck.

"But hey!" Sean said. "You're Mohawk's holding up great!" Sean flashed him a wide smile below bright eyes, gave him two thumbs up and then buried his face in his hands. "What the fuck are we going to do?"

"It'll be all right," Zac said. He stood and stretched his arms. He walked over and leaned against the ropes. He was surprised at how tight they were, how they felt more like steel cables than the rubber-bands he had always imagined them to be. This was life, he thought. Life was tight and full of surprises. He was alive and if he was alive he needed to be a little more lively. He needed to drink and fuck and kick some ass.

Zac put his cigarette between his lips and dashed across the ring, leaping the screaming turtle and causing Sean to roll out the way. He turned at the last moment and put his full weight into the ropes on the other side. The ropes stretched and groaned and then shot him back across but he had not accounted for the force of the reaction and barreled directly over Sean and into Raven, whose leg kicked out and knocked over the screaming turtle, sending ashes and mashed-out cigarette butts across the canvass in a shotgun spread.

"Fucking amateur!" called out a squeaky voice. Zac pushed aside Raven's hair to see Steele waddling with his bowed and hitched stride towards them. He had put on a pair of tight cut-offs and a fresh layer of tanning oil. "Clean that shit up and let me show you how it's done, bubba."

Zac and Raven quickly untangled themselves though not without an apology on the part of Zac and the worry that he might have broken some of her bones. Raven enjoyed, for the briefest of moments, being on her back, some of Zac's weight upon her, the musty smell of him and the feel of his skin to her fingers.

"We really need to practice, Steele," Sean said, pulling himself up to his hands and knees and beginning to scoop up some of the scattered butts. "What the fuck time is it?"

"Time to get that hot little bitch to sing something," Steele said, marching up the metal steps and bowing himself through the ropes. "She's got a nice ass but," he put his hands on his hips and laughed. "Can she sing? I mean, she talks like she's a little kid. Just rub that shit in," he said pointing to the ashes Zac was piling into his palm. "Hell of a lot worse has been spilled in here." He turned his wide, reconstructed smile to Raven and gave her a sly wink. Raven put a scoop of spent cigarettes in the screaming turtle, waited for Sean to do the same and then picked it up and slid out of the ring.

"You don't want to play?" Steele said to her.

"Fuck off," she replied and went to go set the ashtray down on one of the tables Steele used to practice crashing into.

Steele shrugged and raised his eyebrows in a kindly and sympathetic way to Zac and Sean. "All right, boys," Steele said kicking off his flip flops. "This is how you run the ropes!" Steele sniffed, wiped his nose and then bolted from one side of the ring to the other, the ropes yielding to his application of force and momentum. "You lean into them and then transfer the weight! See! See how I'm doing this! And then…" he said, hit the ropes, shot out.

Zac, stupidly, did not realize Steele would aim for him until he was buckled and crumpled to the canvas with a flying cross block.

"Now," said Steele to Sean, resting on Zac's chest, pinning his left arm with his legs and his right with his hands so that all Zac could see was Steel's tightly rippled torso and the skylight above, "there are a number of possibilities from this position." Steele smelled like a chemical approximation of pine trees and ocean breeze.

Zac tried kicking out with his legs but Steele was too tightly wrapped around his arms and positioned too high to be moved in such a way. Zac tried setting his feet and pushing up, arching his back but it had been two years since he'd done any serious lifting and only managed to roll Steele ever so slightly more onto his own face.

"Calm down there, bubba," Steele said. "Just relax and I promise not to break anything." Steele looked back up at Sean. "See, I could take this that I've got here and push it this way…"

The pain shot from Zac's wrist up to his armpit, a wrenching scream that foretold the imminent snap of a bone if the pressure continued. His eyes clenched shut, his teeth grated against each other but he did not cry out.

"…But I promised not to break anything." Steele relaxed the hold and the pain subsided. Zac tried to breathe. "I could also do that with my legs," he said and there was a moment between the saying of it and the doing of it in which Zac came to the realization of what was about to occur and felt the horror of not being able to prevent it. Steele turned and twisted his legs and again the pain came, though this time, due to the nature of the pressure, it seemed to Zac that his elbow was about to be popped off and sent flying out of the ring to bounce off the tin walls and come to rest in the dusty corner and there to shrivel and be forgotten until one of the dogs discovered it, gnawed on it for a bit and then buried it in the back where the ants would find it and bring it bit by bit by bit back to their mound to feed their queen.

Steele released the hold, placed a hand on Zac's chest and pushed himself up. He stood, flexed and laughed.

"Come on up, bubba," he said to Zac and held out his hand.

Zac did not want to be helped up. He wanted to lie there and stay there. Before he got big, James used to hold him down, or sit on his chest or lift him up and toss him into the couch and Zac had hated the helplessness of it, and hated that Lori would come and rescue him. When he was eight and Lori wasn't around, James had come at him once, laughing and growling, and Zac had kicked him in the nuts and ran away and tried to lock himself in the closet, but there was no lock, and James had eventually pried the door open, punched him three times and then shoved him back in. Then he slid the dresser in front of the door, and Zac had to wait three hours for his mom to come home and set him free. By that time, he'd cried out all of his tears and peed his pants. When his dad found out, he gave James the belt and then locked him in the closet for the night to sit in the pee stink and think about what he'd done.

"Come on, bubba," Steele said, still holding out his hand. "Ain't no shame in it. I'm a professional. Did that move on the Mountain Man and he's a hell of a lot bigger than you."

Zac extended his arm and Steele lifted him up with a grimaced smile, the bulging of muscles and the popping of veins.

"Now," Steele said, rubbing his hands together. "Who wants to learn how to fly off the top rope? Sean?"

"Hell, yeah!"

Sean scrambled to his feet and turned around in the ring like a distracted squirrel until Steele directed him to one of the corners and told him to wait while he showed him what to do. Steele slipped through the ropes and then climbed up, using the post to help balance himself. He placed his feet on the ropes and then stood.

"This here is the Five Star Frog Splash," he said. "The trick is to land flat."

Steele bounced and vaulted from the ropes, snapped his elbows and knees together in mid-leap then spread out again as he smacked into the canvas, bounced and landed on his feet. He waved at Sean. "Your turn!"

Sean scrambled out and up and stood on the ropes just as Steele had done.

"Remember," Steele called to him. "Flat. One bounce is good. Two or more ain't."

Sean nodded his head. The mat seemed much further down there than he had thought it would be and the concrete floor outside of the ring seemed perilously close. Somehow he was going to hit the canvas and bounce right out of the ring onto the floor. And then a pile of steel sculptures would fall on him. And then the building would explode.

"Come on, bubba!"

"You can do it," Zac added.

147

Sean bent his knees and thrust himself into the air. He saw the ribs of the building flash by in the distance. He pinched his arms and knees together and then flailed out as the mat came rushing at him. He hit. He bounced. He bounced again. His face slid across the canvas. He thought he heard something snap. He couldn't breathe. Someone had stuffed a blanket down his throat. Someone was laughing. Two people were laughing. He managed to look up. He saw Raven. She wasn't laughing. She was looking at a long-haired dude in a curled-up black cowboy hat, torn black t-shirt and skin-tight black leather pants who had just wandered in.

The dude started sidling over to the ring. "Hey, Steele! Where do we set up?"

"What the fuck?" Sean managed to wheeze out.

"Over near the kids' shit!" Steele said. "We'll clear out more space!" Steele pointed at Raven as she slunk towards the wall. "That's the chick I was telling you about."

The skinny dude in the skinny pants regarded Raven and said, "Cool." He nodded from beneath his curled up black cowboy hat and behind his long hair and said, "We'll talk after the show, babe." He turned and called outside. "Back it up here, man!"

The skinny dude stepped aside as a small moving van sized truck backed into the warehouse. It was painted black and on the side had been spray painted RhinoTooth in classic metal lettering with cold steel coloring above a picture of a fanged rhinoceros playing a double-forked guitar with flames and roses bursting in the background.

"Steele!"

Steele looked down at Sean. "What?" he said.

"What the fuck?"

Steele shook his shoulders which jiggered up into his neck and trembled across his head. "What?' he said.

Sean lifted his chest from the mat. "This is our party, man."

"Technically," Steele said, heading towards the ropes, "this is my party and," he said, ducking under the top one and scissor stepping between them, "as you guys pretty much suck…" He stood outside the ropes, holding the top one and leaning back. "Well…"

"But I got your coke, man," Sean said.

"And for that, I'm still gonna let you play. But after you guys play, we'll let the pros take over, okay? And it will be one fucking rocking party." And with that, Steele did a back flip off the apron, landed lightly on his feet and went to help RhinoTooth set up.

10.

"Do you know any of these people?" Zac asked Raven.

She was putting black eye-liner on him. He could see down her loose shirt if he wanted to but after the first glance he didn't want to. There just wasn't much to see. And she smelled like wet dog. And as she dragged the eye liner pencil across his eye lids he was sure she was going to slip and blind him.

"Some of them," she said. His eyes had golden flecks in them, little floating leaves of autumn but she noticed they never looked at her. His face seemed to take up too much space. And he smelled like sour cabbage. If this were Kitten doing this, she'd probably be straddling him. They'd both probably be naked and she'd be putting on the eye-liner while she was bouncing on his dick but Kitten was nowhere to be found and she'd remembered they were supposed to put eye-liner on him and she'd asked him if he wanted her to do it and he'd said that was okay. Which was about all he ever said. Half the time he mumbled. "You?"

"No." He took a sip of the faintly colored but drinkable beer that had magically appeared along with stacked packages of blue plastic cups, bags of chips, a bowl of dip and a cheesecake brought by a gaggle of teased-out, bleach-blonded girls in shiny spandex who draped themselves over the couches, the tables, Steele and the members of RhinoTooth. They were followed shortly thereafter by a few of Sean's friends, skater dudes and girls caught in the backwash of new wave spikes and whatever was happening next who hung out in a cluster by the ring. The two groups didn't mingle until Steele indicated to the rhythm guitarist of RhinoTooth that Sean had whatever they wanted and, as was common throughout history, commerce bridged cultural divides.

He tried to look around. Dozens more arrived, a pack of skins, a gothic trench coat brigade, a clown car full of long hairs and a van of muscle-laden meat-heads until the cavernous tin structure reverberated with the din of aimless conversation and wanton revelry. Tobacco and pot smoke hung thick in the air, and the stink of it melded with the odor of flesh and second-hand cologne. It evoked the perfumed fetes of the Sun King and the orgies of Nero. Zac looked at Raven's chin. It was smooth and strong. There was a sheen to it, something sleek, and something crumbly at the corner of her lip.

She stood up. "All done," she said.

"Thanks," Zac said. Now his eyes felt surrounded as his fingers felt slathered as his hair felt encased. "You've got something on your lip. In the corner."

Raven touched her tongue to something creamy and sweet. She turned her head and wiped at the little smudge as Sean emerged from the mingling mass.

"Dudes," he said. "Sold all of the coke except for a little something-something we be saving for later. Let me just say RhinoTooth are very generous. Pot's almost all gone. Acid and X sales been a bit sluggish but it's getting to that point in the partying when unwise decisions are about to be made."

Zac shook his head as he took a slug from his blue plastic cup. Raven eyed the spot under the ring where she'd hid the cheesecake and bottle of vodka she'd swiped while the Rhino Tooth singer did a tequila shot off of one of the spandex girl's tits.

"You guys the opening band?"

Sean, Zac and Raven turned. Iggy Pop was standing in front of them. His skin was tanned and leathery, his face long and loose, his jeans were tight and his shirt was off but it wasn't Iggy Pop. Iggy Pop didn't have a belly that fell over his belt. Iggy Pop's hair wasn't falling out. Iggy Pop wasn't missing two teeth.

"I'm Max the Sound Guy. You the opening act?" Max did spit when he talked, just like Iggy Pop.

"We're Double Murder Suicide," Sean said.

"Great name," Max said. "We need to do a sound check."

152

"Okay," Sean said.

Max looked at Sean. He looked at Raven. He looked up at Zac.

"Where's the singer?" he said.

Sean lit a smoke.

"I'll check out back," Sean said.

"I'll check the front," Zac added.

Raven looked up. "Do you think she went up to the loft?"

Sean raised a dark eyebrow over his blue eye. "Doubt it, but..."

"I'll check," said Raven, though she didn't relish the thought of entering the lion's den, or the python's lair or the rhino's hut or whatever idiotic name he would surely have for it.

"Let's rock this shit," Max the Sound Guy said. He raised a devil's horns to the sky.

As Sean bounced and pinged his way through the crowd to the back door and Zac parted the human sea with his arm towards the front. Raven followed him out to put her bag in car. After locking it up she wove her way back through the crowd, craning her neck around, hoping to find Kitten slinking about but there was no sign of her so she made for the stairs up to Steele's loft. She nodded at a boy and girl she knew from the record store who were placing little tabs of paper on each other's tongues. They gave her a smile and asked when she would be on? She said ten minutes and then, glancing around to see if she was being watched, moved like an afternoon shadow up the dusty, concrete steps to a landing, a burnished metal door with a roaring tiger's maw welded to it and a snake shaped handle where a doorknob should be.

She looked back quickly to see that no one was following her and pulled, and then pushed the handle. The door swung in and she slid through, pushing the door closed behind her. What first struck her was the aquarium along the far wall. It must have been thirty feet long, five feet high and cast a deep blue tint over the entire space. Fish of all sorts and sizes, all colors and stripes, made their way along its length, turned with familiar disappointment, and made their way back the other direction, having forgotten the previous trip or the hundred thousand before that, cherishing grand hopes of escape.

As she moved towards the tank, she noticed the kitchen to her right, a projection TV set up in the corner, a square of leather couches and suede chairs surrounding an open fireplace whose flume had been constructed to resemble a dragon's mouth. She noted one of Steele's heavy ugly maces resting in a crudely welded stand on burnished metal table. She caught sight of a king-sized, tiger-striped waterbed above which a four-foot long, foot-wide cock protruded from the wall with steel balls slung in a barbed wire mesh below.

However, as her proximity to the tank and the hundreds of little scaly lives that it contained absorbed her attention, she failed to note the five skylights over her head, the bathroom door near the bed, the spiral staircase up to the roof, nor that she was no longer alone in the room.

Beyond the blinking towers of downtown, the last reach of burning red and orange light failed and gave way to the deepest of blues and then inky black.

Kitten had climbed the fire escape to elude the dogs and found a deck with a small garden, where cucumbers, watermelons and jalapenos grew. The deck had been built on the roof in a space surrounded by skylights, like a little island over a bubbling lake. There was a door she assumed led down to Steele's loft, a table that resembled the spider over the gate, with spindle chairs, and two loungers with red cushions and clawed feet. From one of these loungers, Kitten watched the sun's fiery funeral for the better part of an hour. She tried to capture its burning heart in the cigarettes she pressed to her gloveless flesh but the pain would not free her. She tried twiddling with her piercings, rearranging the ones in her lips, exchanging a few with those in her ears, but that didn't help. She tried masturbating to the visions of the gods of old as they flung off their togas and fucked like wildfire in the heart of the sun, but though she worked her fingers vigorously across her studded clit and probed them deeply within, she just couldn't get going. She ate a jalepeno and wept seering tears as the solar orgy burned out like paper. She was left to stare into the sky, count the few stars that peeked out from beyond the veil, and wonder when they would start without her and what she would do about it.

The skylights took on an alien blue glow and increased the sensation that she was adrift. It was not an unfamiliar sensation. It was not unlike being bounced around in the padded back of a white van then strapped to a gurney and rolled down a hall. Men in white held her down while women in white removed her gloves and her clothes and all of her newly acquired piercings and searched her cavities. She'd been given a thin robe with no back and placed inside a small room with white walls, a white bed, a white toilet and a small white table. She remembered the screams. They filled every hour. She came to know the moods of her fellow patients by the tenor of their screams. She knew when they were hungry. She knew when they were sad or tired or simply scared. It seemed she could still hear them. It was more like a screech, really, when she came to think about it, and then it came again, from below. Kitten leapt to her feet and darted to the nearest skylight. She peered down into the dim blue glow and saw a shadow moving, heard the screech again and saw an oily figure pouncing after it.

Raven hadn't heard him until his thick hands were on her shoulders and his rank breath was on her cheek.

"Welcome to the Tiger's Lair," he'd said, but she hadn't heard him properly because she'd screamed and jumped, smashed into the aquarium and stumbled to the floor.

"What?" she said.

He hoisted her, his thighs flexing, his pecs popping, to her feet and pulled her close.

"I said, 'welcome to the Tiger's Lair, little bird,'" and he said it with a sparkling smile.

Raven felt a wave of nausea. Either the smile or the cologne or the swelling in his shorts or the cheesecake made her want to puke. His left arm clamped her bones to his flesh while his right hand reached up and brushed a strand of white hair back from her dark eyes.

"You sure can move those fingers, doll. You ever play Steele guitar?'

"Why do you have to be such an asshole?" Raven said.

"Hey," he said, pressing her closer, dropping his free hand to knead at his crotch. "Picasso was never called an asshole." His mouth reached up to suck at her face.

She tried to drive her knee into his nuts but he twisted his pelvis away and laughed. He shoved her back. She screeched and fell over a leather chair. She scrambled to her feet but he was on her again, pressing his oily flesh to her, dragging her towards the bed.

She screeched but he giggled.

She bit but he laughed.

She kicked and squirmed. "No!" she yelled. "No!" she yelled at him and "No!" a hundred times she yelled at herself. She'd escaped this a dozen times before. She'd fought this off from pageant officials and guitar heroes. She'd diverted and distracted boyfriends and country club beaus. She'd been waiting for just the right moment, for magic and moonlight, and none of it could be this.

He tossed her on the bed and she felt it roll, heave and swell. She heard the water glump and glomp within. She tried to roll but the waves enveloped her and would not let her escape.

He was dropping his shorts and massaging his little prick to its fullest attention.

"Please," she said. Tears welled up, water beneath her and water above. She hated the word and having to use it. "Please don't, I've never..."

He crawled onto her.

"Then let me show you how it's done, little bird. Let the tiger unleash the phoenix inside you," he said.

158

She felt his stiff little penis against her panties, the final barrier, the thin fabrics that held it back. His chin pressed against her chest, pinning her to the rolling bed and his hands were working their way down to remove the vestiges of what she admitted to herself was a feeble defense.

"You better make it last you son-of-a-bitch!" She looked him dead in the eyes. "Because after you're done I'm going down to my car, getting my gun, I'm going to come back up here and blast your fucking brains out! I'm going to make you say, 'Please', and then I'll pull the trigger." She saw, for a moment, his cheap façade fall. She saw the clapboard panels crack, the shingles crumble, the floorboards start to cave. But then he giggled again.

"Girls and guns," he said. "That's cute."

As her panties were slid down, she closed her eyes and pictured blood and brains upon the floor

Sean couldn't find Kitten but had located a few of his friends out back talking to a girl who claimed to have a third nipple but was refusing to prove it. He was on the verge of convincing her that a private screening would settle the debate when Max the Sound Guy found him.

"Dude!" he said. "I need to set some fucking levels!"

"Max," Sean said. "You realize this girl might have a third nipple?"

"Kid," Max the Sound Guy said, "when I was on tour with White Lion I saw a girl with four tits and a cock ring. Now let's get inside and do this shit."

Zac couldn't find Kitten out front but, after wandering around a bit, peering into a car or two, having a smoke or two, he did run into his sister and Kyle and Del coming through the gate. Del looked smoking hot in a floral summer dress while Lori wore light green shorts and a white blouse. Kyle held a six-pack.

"Hey," Zac said, and, "Hey," Lori replied.

"Where's Sean?" Del said.

"Out back,' Zac said and pointed.

Del danced off. Lori looked around and said it looked like quite the party and asked if his band had played yet. He said they were just about to. She took two beers from Kyle and asked him to wait inside for her. Kyle wandered toward the open doors. She handed one of the beers to Zac and opened her own with a twist. Zac popped his open and took a long slurp. It was better beer than what was in the keg, and it was cold.

Lori looked towards the open doors and Kyle waiting there and then back at Zac. "I don't want us to fight," she said. "Kyle and I talked. Don't make that face…"

"Sorry," Zac said.

"We talked and he said you need to deal with what happened in your own way and I needed to deal with it in mine." She cradled the bottle in both hands. "I need to make order out of chaos and you need to make chaos out of order." She took another drink. "But I love you and I don't want to lose you too. You understand?"

Zac felt sorrow and loss rise within him, like an empty bowl filling up. He wanted to believe her. Maybe if he believed in her sadness, he'd find his own. He'd seen behind the curtain. Still he felt bad because his sister felt bad, and so he felt bad for her. She didn't want him to die or disappear because then she would feel worse, even though it was all bullshit. Sorrow was a sour thing, a growth inside him turned brown and moldy.

The mace slid from Kitten's hand. It went thunk on the floor.

"Is he dead?"

"I don't know. You should go."

"Is he dead?"

"I don't know. Tell Sean I'll be right there."

Raven found her way downstairs then she found the bottle of vodka she'd stashed under the wrestling ring. As she wiped her face she noticed Max the Sound Guy giving her the eye.

"I think they're starting without you," Kyle called out from the doors. The next moment they heard the whine and call of a guitar amp being turned on, and then the thump and rumble of a drum.

"I gotta go," Zac said. He hustled towards the doors.

"Have a good show," Lori called after him. Zac stopped and looked down at Kyle.

"Just be nice to her, alright?" he said.

"That's what I'm here for," Kyle replied.

Zac frowned but there was nothing to be done about it now because Raven was strumming out some chords, Sean was snapping the high-hat and rolling across the toms and Max was waving frantically at him from a table in the back.

Called from the corners and the crevices they came, the bald and the bleached, the drugged and the drunk, they came. They shuffled, skipped, tripped and slumped. They took drags of their smokes and spit on the floor. They made a rough-semi circle in front of the band, crowding the open space between the stage and the wrestling ring. Zac could see them all, maybe a hundred punks, stoners, metal heads, sluts, skaters, posers, strippers, party girls, fashion boys, fags, dykes, divas, long hairs, skin heads, runaways and rejects, staring at him, waiting for the thing that is the something that is supposed to happen.

162

Zac crossed the void between performers and audience and stepped over to his amp. He set the beer on top, hefted the bass by the neck, slid the strap over his shoulder and let it sag into position. He snapped the cord in and then flipped the power switch to the amp and stepped away. He grabbed a pick from a small pile next to the beer and went one-two-three-four over the heavy strings. He looked over at Raven who was standing and staring at a space on the floor in front of her feet. If a white sheet could be bleached beyond white that is how she looked.

"You okay?" he said.

She looked up. There was far and away in her stare, endlessness in the way her mouth formed the word, "What?"

"Test the mic!" a voice boomed out of the monitor. Zac looked to the back to see Max waving his naked arm and pointing at the microphone at the front of their little set-up.

Zac stepped to the mic. He felt raw, like skin that had just had a bandage removed, and painfully conscious of the air. He felt naked, like everybody could see through the cracks of his boots and tell him he needed to clip his toenails. He felt. Like he couldn't wait. Like he would burst.

"Test 1-2" he said. "Test Test."

Max the Sound Guy gave a thumbs up and then a devil's horns. Zac turned around to Sean.

"We'll do the third song first," Sean said. "Just make some shit up until Kitten gets here." He whomped his bass drum three times.

Zac turned to Raven. Her eyes came to focus as she looked to the stairs heading up to the loft and saw Kitten coming down. Raven took a long deep breath. Her fingers tightened and relaxed. She nodded up at Zac.

"Get out the way, motherfuckers!"

The masses parted before her and Kitten marched to the stage with a growl in her step.

"The first song," she said quietly to Raven and then to Sean. She had to tilt her head back to look up at Zac. "The first song," she said to him with a smile full of wickedness and sin. She pulled the mic down to her red red lips as Max swore and frantically adjusted the faders. In a voice that didn't sound like bubblegum at all, a voice that sounded like razor blades and burning cherry ends she said, "We're Double Murder Suicide and this song is called *Fuck Me Open*."

11.

The set began with thunder and ended in a downpour.

"Fuck Me Open" started in a deep rumble before Raven peeled in
and Kitten wailed. Sean pounded at his drums with spastic fury as Zac
filled the underbelly with cardiac currents. Raven and Kitten found the
rhythm of new lovers, pulling and pushing, lost in their own world of sweat
and saliva, flailing about but rising to ecstasy all the same.

Zac chanced a glance at the crowd. Heads were bobbing, fingers
were flexing but there was no moshing, or dancing or hands in the air. They
stood transfixed, paralyzed, trying to process. This was a music unfamiliar
and yet inevitable. There were echoes of days gone by, of basements in
New York, of warehouses in LA and barges along the Thames. This wasn't
punk because Raven ripped. It wasn't metal because Sean didn't do
flourishes or rolls, he simply smashed and crashed. Zac brought the melodic
sensibility of London Goth but these were no delicate vampire bites but the

ripping and tearing of wolves on the moor. Kitten was the banshee call at the center of it all, a dirty little pixie throwing chunks of lava from the bottom of a deep, dark well.

"Fuck Me Open" gave way to "Rubber, Blood and Cum" which moved the kids out of their stupor and sent them swirling to a hurricane of mashing and moshing. It was amidst this storm, in the swirl and rain of a human hurricane that Zac felt his heart pumping its rabid pulse through his hands and Sean made two hundred feet dance on hot coals. Raven peeled off a hundred sweat and dripping water soaked shirts and licked them in the private places that made them sigh as Kitten dipped a poison barb inside their souls and let it liquefy before sucking it out with a triple-twister fun straw. Double Murder Suicide was lost and gone as one, they were the screaming shadows in the swamps, they were the sludge exploding from the sewers beneath to wash away the dust crust covered streets.

"Rubber, Blood and Cum" gave way to "Pink Eye" which rose from the muck on tattered dirty wings and soared into the crying night. Lifting his face to the heavens, Zac could feel the raindrops. Then he realized he was feeling raindrops. He opened his eyes. He saw the water falling in soft crystal beads. They were dancing on Sean's drums and bursting open on the back of Raven's neck.

Kitten looked up. She opened her caged mouth wide and licked her tinsel stained lips.

166

"This next song," she said, "is Steelehead."

The opening verse of the song wondered if fish could fly or do they just flop around and die? How does it feel to taste a fistful of steel? The answer to these questions stumbled down the steps naked, wet and bleeding, clutching his mace in hand.

"What the fuck?" some dude said. Several others asked if he was alright but he shoved them aside, stumbled, recovered and made for the girl with the black satin gloves, the red skirt, black tights and black boots, the girl with all that silver in her face, the one that was looking right at him and laughing.

Kitten laughed because he looked so ridiculous. He was some dwarfish Grendal with his bobbing little prick. She laughed because the overhead lights cast deep shadows in the caves of his eyes and the eyes themselves were so desperately intent on her demise. If only he knew what she did to men such as he. If only he'd read the news articles from ten years ago, about a girl who shot her dad with his own gun. She giggled as blood oozed from the side of his skull and poured from his nose. She thrust her chin in the air as drips of water splashed her cheek, as he raised his mace in a trembling arm, growled something that sounded something like, "my fish", and swung wildly, missed completely and fell face first into the drum kit.

Sean fell off his stool trying to get out the way. Raven stood holding the last note on her fingers. Zac unslung his bass as Steele thrashed and flailed amidst the falling brass and skins.

"Hey…," Steele started to say but it didn't come out right. It sounded like the dumb girl Kitten used to steal desserts from in the psych ward. Steele had that same dumb look and that same slow slide to anger.

"Hey!" Steele said again, clearer now. He stood and reached out a clutching claw towards her. He raised his mace once again and then his face was broken by the back of Zac's bass. Kitten heard the crack of small bones snapping as the reverb went howling.

Zac was twelve when James said he needed to borrow Zac's baseball bat. When Zac asked why, James said there are no rules in a street fight. The next day, Zac had to use another kid's bat at practice because James had left Zac's broken and bloody in a ditch.

Zac was sixteen when he pulled around the end and led a convoy for his running back. Twenty yards later and the back was streaking down the sideline, untouched and un-pursued save for himself and a solitary defender a few steps behind Zac. The impulse was nasty and unnecessary. Zac turned, ducked his head, raised up at impact and flipped the kid ten feet in the air. He landed with a crumple. The cheers caught in throats. His coach was happy.

Zac stood over Steele, his instrument broken, the body hanging by four strings.

"Fuck," Sean said. He got to his feet. Raven still couldn't move. He looked at Kitten just in time to see her face light up with criminal pleasure before the sky opened and rage poured through.

The first meathead yelled and charged, swinging wild. Zac dropped the bass, grabbed the dude's head and swung the stupid bull into a pack of skinheads who took to the occasion the way a troop of cub scouts might to a bag of marshmallows. A second meathead charged and struck a glancing blow to the side of Zac's head and then arced a left hook that caught him in the gut. Air rushed from his lungs. Zac dropped to a knee but threw a quick uppercut to the meathead's nut sack before he was buried under a pile of long haired metal dudes.

A pack of taloned harpies reached out for Kitten. They tore at her flesh and spit at her eyes but she fought them fiercely, kicking, screaming and biting.

Raven got knocked out of her stupor by the maelstrom of combat as she was shoved into her amp stack and then over it with a wail of feedback to accompany her fall.

Then things got out of hand.

The first meathead was being kicked and stomped by a dozen Doc Martins until two of his meathead buddies arrived to save him, scattering the skinheads. Three members of RhinoTooth fought off some skaters who were attempting grievous bodily harm to their keyboard. Kyle grabbed Lori who grabbed Del and got out of there as a half-dozen of the peroxide brigade launched a pitched hair-pulling battle with a handful of biker dykes, while a small squadron of fashion boys screamed and ran for their lives. Max the Sound Guy got up on the ring apron and shouted for everyone to chill until some suburban preppie smacked him in the back of the head with a chair and he fell through what was left of the table holding the chips and dips.

Heedless of his own personal safety, Sean embarked on a rescue and recovery mission. He found Kitten first, pulling her off one of the spandex sisters. Blood covered her mouth and poured from her nose, but she was laughing wildly and spitting fury, trying to get back on top of the girl and finish pounding her head into the cement, which was dappled wet

170

by the sweat and blood and water dropping from the ceiling. Both she and Sean heard a roar and saw a long haired boy go flying over their heads. Zac rose from the pile. His face was a crimson mask, his shirt torn from his shoulders, and fire blazing in his dark eyes even as he was swarmed by a third wave of meat and metal.

Sean tried to push toward him but felt his progress hindered. Someone was reaching at his pouch. He let go of Kitten, clutched at the strap and cursed when, with a shriek, he felt the buckle snap and the pouch get pulled away as a body fell on top of him. He wailed as paper bills and snowy powder filled the air. Hands that had just been reaching for throats now clutched at $20 bills, little bags of grass, paper tabs, a Big Mama Lighter, some throat drops and a dozen various and sundry things. Sean kicked and shoved his way out from under the person who had landed on him and scrambled on the floor like an angry spider, grabbing at every little pill and crumpled bill he could find. He spat at the thieving bastards, clawed and punched at them, but they would not give up their bounty. They slapped him and kicked him and sent him reeling to the ground again, and then two gloved hands pulled him up and pushed him towards the door.

Zac understood that sad and sordid acts occur at the bottom of a pile. Good natured boys who wouldn't normally think of shoving their thumbs into someone's eye socket clutched and twisted nut sacks, raked

171

skin with sharpened nails and even invaded cavities they had no business exploring --- but this was no scramble for a loose football. This was tooth and nail, fist and claw. He felt something pop in his hand and heard a child's scream. The body that had been on top of him twisted away. He shoved his way to his feet. The violence within him was sheer and total. His only thought was of inflicting pain. The red god of war had invaded him until, looking down at the thing in his hand, he recognized it as an ear. He saw the boy on the ground, his hands covering a hole in his head. Zac snapped back to a world of clean air and Christmas morning photographs. He bent down and pressed the ear into the boy's clutching hands.

"Sorry," he said. He saw Kitten leading Sean out of the warehouse and waded after them. The meatheads had regrouped, spotted Zac trying to flee and gave chase, trampling the innocent in their paths. Even as he made it out and almost reached Sean and Kitten, Zac heard their terrible roars and turned to see their terrible teeth. He readied himself. He saw the world go red again, but then the sky was rent with a thunder clap, and all the savage hearts slowed as crimson shaded eyes turned to regard the dark queen standing on the hood of her slick black 1958 Buick Roadmaster with a big honking gun in her hand.

12.

Her white hair flashed like lightning as smoke trailed from the barrel of the gun. The guitar slung behind her could have been a samurai sword silhouetted as it was by moon gleam. "I am the goddess of art and death, the Morgainne, and the carrion crow." She let the weight of the gun lower her arm. "Everyone go home." She was the wall against which the fever of battle broke.

"All my shit," Sean said as Kitten wrestled with him. "All our shit!"

Zac grabbed him up and tossed him in the back. Raven hopped down from the hood, the gun at her side, her eyes locked on the meatheads and metal boys still frothing.

Kitten did a slow saunter to the passenger side. "Night boys," she said with a little wave of her satin coated fingers.

"Get in the car, Kitten," Raven said.

Kitten obliged with a toss of her hair, a swish of her tail and a purr on her lips.

"You too, Zac."

Zac did as he was told.

Raven felt like she'd been holding ice-cubes under her skin for a very long time. The air pricked at her. She could hear locusts far away. She could taste the smoke and smell the gunpowder as it hung heavy in the air. She opened her door and unslung her guitar, dropping it inside. With a cold iron stare she followed, watching the meatheads seethe while the rest of them, the Goths and the skins, the preps and the pretty ones, the dregs and the diseased slid off into the night. Keeping the gun visible, she started the car, shifted into drive and slowly rolled along the path and under the clawing giant spider gate. She watched in the rear-view mirror for any acts of bravado but none came.

They drove two blocks more before Raven slid the gun back into its holster beneath her seat. One of the first trips she'd made in her new car was to the gun shop, where her father used to take her before their annual trip to the hill country, and then she drove to the firing range, where men in pressed denim shirts and camo hats gave her the eye but otherwise left her in peace. Even if she looked like a skeleton they respected a woman who could handle a firearm.

Sean bounced up and down in his seat. "We have to go back!" he yelled. "All our shit! All our shit's back there!"

Kitten looked around for her bag but it wasn't there.

174

"I left my bag on the roof," she said.

Raven looked down at the floorboards. Hers was where she left it.

"Fuck that shit!" Sean yelled. "You don't understand," he unclenched his hands. He'd managed to salvage two $20's, the $100, a baggie of pot, a pack of rolling papers and the little blue bottle that had eight hits of X in it. "Aldo's going to kill me."

"It's going to be okay," Kitten said. "Does anyone have any smokes?"

"I do," Zac said. "I think." He dug in his pocket for his pack.

"How is it going to be okay?" Sean said.

"We'll figure something out," Raven said. Three blocks away flashing ambulance lights and wailing sirens shot the other way. "We need to get off the street. Get back home. We'll figure something out."

Sean balled the money and drugs up in his fists again. "Great," he said. "You guys figure something out. Meanwhile I'll be in the shower getting my guts torn out by a chainsaw." He clamped his eyes shut against the harsh injustices of the world, balling his fists against his skull against the tragedy of it all. "My fucking kit! I just got that stuff! Godfuckingdamnit!"

Zac pried the pack out his pocket. There were five cigarettes left inside, each and everyone crushed and broken. "Stop whining," he said.

"Fuck you!"

"Fuck you."

"Fuck you twice! What the fuck happened?"

"Steele tried to rape me," Raven said.

Zac held the crumpled pack in his hand. Sean held the remains of his drug dealing empire.

"So I hit him with that big metal thingy he was carrying when he attacked us," Kitten said. "And then I smashed all his aquariums. You should have seen all those fish flopping around."

They passed under 59 and drifted by the convention center that looks like a giant freezer.

"I think I tore some guy's ear off," Zac said.

"What?" Sean and Raven and Kitten all said together.

"Think so. I got out of this pile and had this thing in my hand and looked down and it looked like an ear," Zac said. "All the smokes are busted."

"Gimmie." Sean reached out for the pack. "I've got papers," he said. Zac dropped it in his hand.

Raven looked in the rear view mirror. "What did you do with it? The ear."

"Gave it back to the guy," Zac said.

Sean set the pill bottle, the baggie, the bills, and the pack next to him. "Whose was it?" He ripped a paper out, snatched up the hundred, placed that on his lap and set the paper on top.

176

"Some long haired guy. I thought maybe he could get it sewn back on." Zac laughed. "What the fuck," he sighed.

"Maybe," Sean said. He pried one of the cigarettes out of the pack and pinched out the tobacco onto the paper. "How does that even happen?" Using the hundred, he rolled the paper around the tobacco and sealed it with a lick.

"You pull hard enough and parts come off," Zac said.

"I should have pulled Steele's dick off!" Kitten said. She was turning and twisting and bouncing up and down.

"Here, baby," Sean handed her the smoke. Zac handed her his Zippo. In the fire's light, her wide face looked soft and warm.

Zac hurt everywhere, his face was covered in sticky blood and his heart was having problems slowing down. He could feel the shakes starting in his shoulders as Raven guided them along deserted streets, past empty parking lots and barren sidewalks, and then they were in downtown Houston on a Saturday night and there was nothing to see. The lobbies of the skyscrapers were deserted. The little lunch places and steakhouses were all closed. There were no bars here, no cars and only a grizzled old black man shoving around a shopping cart stuffed with aluminum cans in clear plastic bags. Sean handed him a rolled smoke. Kitten gave him back his lighter. Raven did a little eyeball dance every three seconds, the mirrors, the side

177

streets, the distance listening for sirens, looking for lights. They were a little mobile dynamo blasting through a dead circuit.

"Fuck," Sean said. He lost control of the third cigarette and tobacco flung out everywhere. He needed a pill, something smooth and mellow, something to take the teeth out of his spine. He looked next to him. There was just the X which would do the exact opposite. But at least he'd die happy. He snatched up the bottle and squeeze twisted the top off. His hands were twitching and he felt like ice had wrapped itself around his nuts.

"Dude, you okay?" Zac said.

"Yeah, yeah," Sean said. He managed to pour the pills from the bottle to his palm, only losing two of them down into the seat. "Take one," he said.

"What is it?"

"X."

Kitten practically crawled into the back. "Me! Me! Me!" She opened her metaled mouth wide. Sean snagged one of the little blue pills and popped it. Kitten swallowed and squealed. "One for Raven!" She snatched one, turned and slid it between Raven's lips.

"I've never done X before," Zac said.

Sean looked up at him. "It will make everything all right."

"Better than all right," Kitten said. She plucked another pill from Sean's hand, crawled half-way over the seat, propping herself up with an arm on Zac's thigh and said, "Open the hanger, here comes the trolley!"

She'd gotten it all wrong but Zac opened his mouth anyway and Kitten placed the pill on the center of his tongue.

"Where are we going?" he said.

"My place," Raven said and darted the Buick across Travis St., Main and then Dallas, wound around the historical homestead, and then rolled out to Allen Parkway which swept along Buffalo Bayou, a greasy, toxic twist of a stream that once fed the swamp Houston was built on top of, into which Houston sank an inch or so every year. After a few too few miles the parkway ended at a light. A left turn would take them towards Greenbriar and Sheppared, where they could stop at Nan's Records or have some food at House of Guys. A right turn would take them across the bayou to Memorial and then out to the Galleria where they could go ice skating at the mall. But they were going straight ahead to the oldest, richest neighborhood in town. She waited for it to turn green and then rolled straight through the gates of River Oaks.

Zac sat up. He stared as they passed mansions built on small hills and imagined swimming pools behind their brick walls. "You live here?" he said.

179

"Yeah," Raven sighed because she'd never moved out. She'd grown up in a pink mansion on a dutifully kept green hill, and when she did move out, she didn't go very far, just to the apartment over the garage that some old servant used to live in way back when. Her dad had used it to store legal documents until she'd asked him for the place. Her mother was appalled but by then they weren't really speaking anyway. She'd meant to find a place of her own, some cool apartment in Montrose but at all the places she looked at, she didn't feel safe parking her car.

The live oaks hung low over the streets and driveways, their massive trunks and broad leaves hiding the city and the sky. June bugs buzzed and bumbled about, but otherwise, all was shadow and quiet. The garage door opened and Raven backed the car in with practiced care. She turned off the engine as the wide white door rolled back down.

13.

The bedroom was dark and smelled of moonlight. Ethereal music played on the stereo. A warm glow, the color of cinnamon and sin, flickered from the candles Raven had lit after she dropped her bag on the black Formica table in the front room and placed her guitar in the little stand next to the King sized bed that took up almost the entire room. Like her car, Raven's apartment was tastefully decorated in reds and blacks, with an assortment of talismans, from Mexican crosses to Celtic icons. Sean and Kitten and Zac and Raven lay on the bed staring up at the glow-in-the-dark star stickers Raven had stuck on her ceiling.

"Is that the big dipper or the little dipper?"

"I need a shower."

"I need to pee."

"Am I supposed to feel all tingly?"

"Yes."

"That's the big dipper."

"I feel all tingly and the stars are starting to look like they're going into hyperdrive."

"That's good."

"I need a new shirt."

"I need $1400."

"What's that one?"

"The Goddess."

"Goddess of what?"

"The sky, the earth, love and war."

"So pretty much everything."

"Pretty much."

"I like it."

"I feel like something slick is touching me."

"I'm touching you."

"What are you doing?"

"Just relax."

"Don't…"

"What…?"

"Holy shit," Kitten said.

His brother had tried to warn him. "You're gonna be BMOC," he'd said.

It had started in 7th grade, the first time he'd had to take a group shower, after the first fall football practice. Mike Sawyer was the first to notice it. He'd said, "Holy shit," too. Pretty soon half the team was gathered around Zac. He tried to escape to his locker, wrapping a towel around himself but they followed him and demanded a viewing. After much begging and pleading he finally relented. He would have to take the towel off sometime and he'd have to take more showers anyway.

A collective gasp went through the audience as he removed the towel.

"Can I touch it," Mike said, his hand inching towards Zac.

"No you can't touch it, you fag!" Zac said.

"I just want to see if it's real," Mike said.

"It's real, okay."

"What the hell is going on here?" Coach Wilson yelled. "Why the hell are you little Nancies standing around Gardner like a pack of princess daisies?" Coach Wilson stopped dead at the sight of it. His jaw dropped. "Holy shit!" he said. "Your mama fuck a donkey?"

For weeks afterwards, as he walked down the hall, he heard the whispers and felt the stares. Boys and girls alike would turn beet red at just the thought of such a thing running rampant through their quiet school. He even saw it in the eyes of the teachers, eyes that followed his crotch as he fled their classrooms with his book pressed firmly but not entirely successfully against an unwanted and uncalled for boner that exceeded all attempts at concealment and in the barely stifled laughter of Mr. Bennett in Spanish class when the word 'burro' came up.

From the literature his dad kept under the bathroom sink off his parents' bedroom, Zac had come to understand that he had been granted a great blessing. However, he soon used only the stalls to pee. He took his showers quickly and dressed as fast as he could, practically standing inside his locker, and he never allowed himself to be alone with Ms. Fitch or Mr. Newel.

"Ah, yes," James had said with a proud smile on his face. "The family legacy! Just as your brother, your father, and his father before him," James had declared, "long is our lineage, onto the days of Arthur and his knights, long has our family wielded mighty swords! Be proud, young swashbuckler," he said, wagging his cock in the air, slashing it against invisible foes. "Carry thy staff with honor and it will bring you much pussy!" James bore his point home with a flourish and a final thrust. "And look, you can make a sailboat with it!"

Indeed, his brother had been prophetic. Zac's cock became the ultimate challenge for girls of a certain inclination. In upstairs closets at keg parties, they demanded to see it. They dared each other to touch it. And a few, a brave few, opened themselves to receive it, or as much as they could but none of them could cover it and no condom could contain it so he always ended up beating off in the sink.

184

This type of fame, and such rewards, came with a price, however. Most of the girls at his school were afraid of the thing. And while the rest of the boys were able to keep their privates private, the thing lurking in Zac's cotton covered depths meant his dating life, while occasionally pleasurable, was limited. If there was one thing he was thankful for with James's death, it was that everyone forgot about his dick. It had remained unmolested by outside entities ever since.

They had been lying together so peacefully, shoulder's barely touching, drifting lightly through the cosmos on Raven's bed. Zac had hardly noticed Kitten's hand and where it was headed until it was too late. Now she was turning, twisting, crawling down there.

"Oh my God, Raven, give me your hands!"

"What?" Raven looked up. "Wow," she said.

Sean was bouncing happily between Orion and Cassiopeia when he felt Raven move away from him, slide down the bed and turn towards Zac. He turned on his side and propped his head up with his elbow. "Dude, it's like the Leaning Tower of Penis," he said.

"Thanks," Zac said.

Kitten laughed. "Does it have a name?"

"Donkey," Zac said.

"Oh, right," she said. "I don't like it." She frowned and then smiled. "I'm going to call it Clair."

"Clair?" Sean said.

"It's friendlier that way."

Sean reached out and found an unattended section of Zac to touch, to feel, to make sure it was real. "Hello, Clair," he said.

"Guys," Zac said. "This feels a little weird."

"You never had two girls and a dude stroking Clair before?" Sean said.

"No," Zac said.

Sean slid the tips of his fingers along the main vein. It felt as most pricks did, like a snare drum, the skin stretched smooth and tight. This was just a very big snare drum. "Do me one favor," Sean said.

"What's that?" said Zac.

"No matter what happens in the next hour," Sean said, "do not stick this thing up my butt."

Zac laughed. He rubbed his head against the pillow behind it. He found that rubbing his head on the pillow felt good too. Between the head rubbing and the penis touching every pore, every neuron was on high alert and in danger of reception overload. "I can't make any promises," Zac said.

Sean gripped hard. His fingers would not reach his thumb. "Do NOT do it!"

186

"I don't know, Sean. You got some sweet cheeks."

"And a big DO NOT ENTER sign across them!"

"Both of you shut up!"

Kitten regarded Zac's penis with a well-practiced eye. She had seen big cocks and small cocks, cocks that schlumped off to the right and those that went left. She'd seen one that curled up almost to the guy's tummy and one that forever drooped. She'd seen them tattooed, pierced and one that had been surgically forked like a snake's. But Clair was a thing unto itself. She glanced at Raven. She saw the awe and wonder, the fear and hunger in her eye.

"This is it," she said to her.

"This?" Four hands held it and still there was room for more.

"The goddess demands sacrifice, does she not?"

The muscles rippled across Raven's jaw. "She does."

Kitten pressed her forehead to Raven's cheek. She whispered through grinding teeth. "We have seen battle and blood tonight. We have made the heavens weep and the pagans dance. The time has come. We must prepare."

Sean's own brave soldier had risen to attention, ready for deployment. It was no Goliath but it was no David either. It was the kind of everyday Joe that wins wars and builds nations. "What are y'all doing?"

187

Zac opened his eyes. Something new was happening. Kitten and Raven let go, slid off the bed and stood up.

"The virgin must be cleansed and I really have to pee before we get down to business," Kitten said. "Sean, keep that thing busy." She took Raven by the arm and led her into the bathroom.

Zac looked down at Sean. It was not a position he had even remotely entertained earlier in the day and yet here in this warm world, in this dark corner under these green glowing stars, his skin feeling like wine, it all seemed so right.

Sean looked up at Zac. He had to admit things were looking up. Up and up. Up and down. He heard a toilet flush and then a shower come on. He moved closer to Zac, pulling himself up and over his tree trunk sized leg and nestling between the mountainous thighs that smelled of sweat and other, more pungent aromas. He gripped Clair at the base and thought of the woods behind his old house where the pine trees grew before they all got cut down for a new neighborhood. He remembered standing, looking up, seeing them sway against the blue sky and wanting to rise with them, wanting to tickle the air at the tops of the trees.

Zac took in a slow slash of breath as he felt Sean's tongue slide up the underside of his cock. He felt the long soft hair sweep up his legs. He watched as Sean's dark face rose over the tip and saw the bright eyes open as if dawn awoke to mid-day.

Sean smiled. "I have to try," he said.

Music and blood, an ear, gunshots in the air, a bed covered in bodies, a man's mouth descending, Zac gave into it all, he closed his eyes and fell.

Raven moved her hands over her chest, rubbing her palms over her stiff nipples, feeling the water flow over them and thought how intense it would be if they could shoot lasers. She could run around shooting lasers out of her nipples blasting away aliens. She ran her hands down along her hips, feeling the bones, rubbing them, enjoying them, regretting them, enjoying the water, warm, cascading and Kitten's soapy hands caressing her back, wiping away the grime, polishing up the bones.

Kitten washed every inch of her, from her fingertips to her toes. She took a sponge to the back of her ears and the tops of her knees. She knelt down and scrubbed her heels. She turned her around and used her tongue to clean inside of her. Raven's back pressed against the tiled wall, her hips rose and she thrust herself on Kitten's face. Sheets of orange sherbet rose from deep down below.

14.

Zac was enjoying himself. Sean couldn't get it all the way in but his tapping tongue caused little Vietnamese leprechauns to run up and down his spine while flashbulbs popped behind his eyeballs. Then the music stopped. He opened his eyes to see a little white butt dart back into the bathroom. Sean got off of him and rolled over to the stereo. He traced his finger along the rows of CD's until he found the right one. Zac rose up on his elbows.

"What's going on?"

"Ceremony," Sean whispered. He popped the CD player open, took out the Dead Can Dance that had been droning away and placed Peter Gabriel's *Passion* in. Far away a lonely flute snaked across desert sands.

Raven entered white and thin. Her hair had been brushed back, wet and slick over her skull causing the bones of her face to be even more prominent in the flickering candlelight. The skin that covered her sharp nipples and her naked sex like parchment was nearly translucent, blue veins glistening under lavender oils. She took measured steps to the end of the bed and raised her arms in a crucifix pose.

"This is fucked up," Zac said.

Sean shushed him

Kitten appeared at Raven's side. Her body, in contrast, was solid and firm, her skin pink but butchered. Drums rose from the sands as she crawled onto the bed, and knelt at Zac's hip. Sean shucked off his pants and took the same position on the other side. They held out their hands.

Raven tilted forward, breathing deep so that the ribs spread like wings, she took their hands and moved herself over the implement of transgression. She locked her eyes on Zac and any power he might have had to pull away or warn her that such an act should not be attempted was disintegrated as easily as dandelion puffs before a storm.

Kitten and Sean took hold of the phallus as Raven descended cautiously.

"Wait!" said Sean.

"Motherfucker, what?" Kitten said.

"Does anyone here have AIDS?"

"No, goddamnit!" Kitten said.

"No," said Zac.

"Obviously not," Raven said.

"Good," Sean said. "Me neither. Got tested last week. All systems go. Commence primary coupling!"

"Just breathe," Kitten said.

Raven braced her hands on Zac's chest and he placed his on her knees. He squeezed as she descended, her virgin fold meeting the impossibility of him.

"It's not…" she hissed.

Kitten reached up and spread her wide. Sean pushed her bony butt down as he maneuvered Clair towards her hole. It began to go in.

Raven's hair fell like slick snakes over his face and Zac felt impenetrable resistance. The music and the firelight boiled within him but the way was barred and he feared the consequences of forced entry.

"I can't!" Raven said. Her fingers dug into Zac's chest, her stomach seized, she tried to breathe, to relax, to let the flower she knew to be inside her open in the moonlight but it would not yield. It cried out with the tearing and screamed with the pain.

"Just fucking do it!" Kitten commanded.

"Raven, you don't have to," Zac said.

Her face contorted to a skeletal rage. "Yes, I DO!" She punched at herself. "Open up you stupid pussy bitch!"

"Wait!" Sean said. "We need ice."

Sean busted out of the bedroom and skated over to the fridge in the kitchen. He popped open the freezer and grabbed a half-filled tray of cubes. He snapped and twisted them until they cracked out and then settled back down and then he skipped back into the bedroom. Zac was sitting up, his back against the headboard. Raven sat slumped near his knees while Kitten lay face down, palms up, at the foot of the bed.

"Raven," Sean said, "on your back." He picked out an ice cube.

"Why?" Raven said.

"Trust me," Sean said. He smiled. "Kitten, keep that thing at attention. Zac!"

"What?"

"Stay focused," he said. "Raven, on your back."

"Fine," Raven said and collapsed next to Zac, her shoulder touching his side. She watched as Kitten slithered to the other side of Zac, nestled in under his arm and started playing with his penis.

She hated that stupid Clair! It was like a tree she couldn't climb or a guitar riff she couldn't play. Then the air went out of her and her thoughts of Clair dissipated as a shot of pure white cold struck from the very depths of her. She looked down. Sean was between her legs, sliding an ice cube up in her and then pulling it out, running it around the lips and then in again

193

and she felt the winter blast out to her toes and into the frayed strands of her hair.

Sean withdrew the nearly melted cube and popped the remains in his mouth, lowered his face to Raven and began a little ice dancing routine on her clit with his tongue. Raven's back arched, her neck craned, she gripped at Zac's leg, the ragged black nails biting into his skin.

Kitten snatched the tray and picked out a cube of her own then crawled back up, lay herself across Zac's belly, pining his penis beneath her and began to slide the cube first across Raven's right nipple and then the left. She followed the ice with warm kisses and soft circles.

"I don't want to hurt her," Zac said, putting his filthy hand on her lily white ass.

"Life is pain," Kitten said. "Pain is life." She paused in her attentions to Raven to reach back and wedge his hand between her legs. "If we don't know pain, how would we know joy?"

 Zac slid a finger inside her.

They were, all four, connected like a junior scientist electricity set. Energy surged through them, from fingers to lips to nipples to clits. They were bodies twisted on a bed but this was no funeral pyre but a raft on a storm tossed sea. They were servants to sin, sacrificing the self to communal desire. The music swelled with strings and drums, voices joined to climb on high.

"Now," Raven called. "Now!"

Kitten melted off of her and Sean evaporated from below. Zac rose above her and she opened herself to him. She wanted him to do this to her, he thought. He had to do this because she had to have it done. He closed his eyes. He saw fireflies sparkle. He heaved himself at her. The boundary broke and he was inside of her. Raven screamed. Blood flowed and all and all and everything trembled in the night.

Interlude

After Sean took a shower he found a pair of Raven's black silk panties. He tried them on. He liked the feel of them. He found a tight pink t-shirt with a picture of a bunny done in sequins and a pair of deep black sunglasses. He put them on. He put on his pants and shoes. He was ready to go. Aldo was waiting. He traced the slice on his hand with his other pinkie finger. The superglue was holding it together. He asked Raven if he could borrow $2000.

Kitten put all of her sticky old clothes back on. She went down to the pool, curled up in a chair under a looming oak tree and watched the ribbons of light turn and weave in the water.

Raven owned one white dress. It shimmered. She painted her eyes and drew the goddess symbol for life, woman and war on her cheek bones. She painted her lips red. She brushed out her long white hair and pulled on smooth soled black boots. She told Sean they should stop at Whataburger on the way and she could get him the money on Monday.

Zac showered after Sean. He enjoyed the water on his skin. He turned it very hot and then very cold. Raven gave him one of her baggiest t-shirts. It was black with a square of wavy lines. Above the wavy lines read "Joy Division". Below the lines read "Unknown Pleasures." The sleeves were too tight so he cut them out. He munched on some ice and said they would need to stop for more smokes too.

They stopped for gas and smokes and they each got a cheeseburger on the way to Heaven.

Night

1.

Sean led Kitten, Raven and Zac past the line of chatting cherubs

that had drifted in to town on powdered wings from the monochrome

suburbs, past the slouching devils that had oozed out of the kaleidoscopic

streets and up a cracked set of concrete steps to the gates of Heaven. St.

Peter waited there, a wraithlike man who sat upon a leather stool before a

velvet rope and appraised them with a long suffering eye.

"They're with me," Sean said.

St. Peter nodded, unsnapped the rope and waved them in with a

shriveled hand.

They heaved their way through a heavy door and encountered a

succubus behind an iron grate who would have demanded coin for their

passage but Sean called her Brandy, whispered words of dark delight to her,

and the demoness let them pass with a laugh and a wave. He led them down

a black-lit passage, spinning and bouncing, his teeth flashing green.

Raven's hair glowed like ghost light, as did Zac's socks. Kitten moved invisibly through the maze, only the flecks of skin that had fallen from her hair to her shoulders gave her presence away. Sean shoved open a final metal door and shivered delightedly at the dancing, drinking, smoking, snorting, shooting, sweating, laughing, weeping, spinning, booming, whistling, salivating, whirling, wondering, wandering, and carnal bliss before him.

It was a sensory overload to Zac who thought that after the sex and cheeseburgers, the drug might be wearing off but the sleeping little dragons woke up, they arched their backs and flapped their wings, they swished their tails and spat fire at the primal regions of his brain. He looked up. A girl wearing nothing but glitter and a pair of wings danced in a cage high above.

"I have to go talk to Aldo!" Sean shouted. "Be right back!" He slipped away.

"I have to dance!" Kitten yelled. She took Raven by her thin wrist and dragged her down to the dance floor where they slipped between slithering bodies to the thudding, pumping beats and whistling squeals.

Zac crossed himself as he stared in wild wonder at the angel above and the people below. A DJ spun from where the church choir must have once been. To his right, alcoves had been converted into booths populated by the slickly dressed and the scantily clad. To his left ran a bar and beyond that a door marked EXIT. His mouth felt dry and ashy. He needed ice.

201

Sean found Aldo exactly where he expected him to be, sitting alone in the back booth, wearing, under a white suit, a black silk shirt with the collar open, exposing his smooth skin and an ornate silver cross. With a nod, Aldo invited Sean to sit. Sean began by telling Aldo about the gig and how awesome it went, and how he'd sold all the shit and made all the money, but then about the brawl and what happened with the pouch, and the money, for which he was really, really sorry and how Raven had gotten them out by shooting her gun, and how she would loan him the cash on Monday. He would have told Aldo about going back to Raven's place but Aldo held up his hand, indicating that Sean should shut up

Manny appeared at the table. Aldo nodded towards the back. Manny touched Sean's shoulder, made a similar nod in the same direction, and waited for Sean to slip out of the booth. Sean followed Manny to a pair of black doors. Manny pushed them open and ushered Sean down a wood-paneled hallway. As the doors closed behind him, the music softened from thrashing and pounding to a dull rhythmic thud. At the far end of the hall there loomed a black metal door with a snap lock and a FIRE EXIT sign that Sean briefly contemplated dashing towards. They passed two closed doors and then an open one where a balding man hunched over a desk, scribbling notes in a ledger and tapping keys on a calculator. Sean saw all manner of papers tacked to the walls, and a photograph of a man holding up a large fish.

Manny opened the final door before the fire exit. Sean stepped in. The small stained glass windows along the top of the wall indicated that this room had once been a private chapel, now converted into a private lounge. A red velvet banquette ran around three sides beneath dimly glowing golden sconces. There were two tables that could be moved as needed. A small bar was against the wall next to the door. Several ash trays were placed about. There appeared to be no signs of barrels, bullwhips or jell-o.

Zac slid a cube of ice around his mouth as he stared up at the angel in the cage. He moved the frozen water along the inside of his cheek as he watched her thighs slide against each other and the feathers of her wings cascade with color. He rubbed the back of his head against the carpeted pillar. He couldn't stop smiling or feeling the smile inside of himself, pushing out his ribs, tickling his kidneys.

Raven and Kitten slithered against each other. The final feathers of youth had molted, Raven thought as she danced. Turning and letting her arms flow out, then curling in, wrapping up Kitten, smoothing her fur and letting her go. She felt good. She felt fine. She'd eaten a whole cheeseburger on the way to Heaven. She hurt. She ached. She had bled. It was like they still echoed inside her, Kitten's rough tongue, Sean's sure hands and Zac's donkey.

Sean sat on the banquette, his feet tapping along to the beats he could feel through the walls. He leaned forward, his elbows resting on one of the tables, and smoked his third cigarette since Manny led him in here and told him to wait. He really wanted a cup of ice, to feel it slip and slide across his tongue just as Raven had a few hours before. He'd already investigated the bar and found it empty. He'd thought of skipping down the hall to raid the ice machine but Manny had said not to leave the room. So he waited. Feeling good. Feeling happy. His toes wouldn't stop tapping. He tapped to the beat and remembered he was supposed to have gotten new shoes as the door opened and Manny held it for Aldo to enter.

"Hey, Aldo," Sean said. He sat up straighter and mashed his cigarette out. "There any water in here?"

Manny closed the door and Sean and Aldo were left quite alone. Aldo brushed at his sleeve, turned to his left and went and sat on the banquette some feet from Sean. He put his hands to his head and leaned forward. He took a long deep breath, lifting his head and leaning back. He held it. Released it.

"Take off the sunglasses," Aldo said.

Sean slipped them off and placed them on the table in front of him.

Aldo did not look at him but at something on the far wall.

Sean slid a little towards him.

"It was a crazy scene, Aldo..." Sean hopped an inch closer, pressing his hands into red fabric. He felt the stains in the fabric. He felt the smoothness where a sticky fluid had been smeared. He felt the char where a smoldering ash had been hastily beaten out.

"Aldo..." he said. Everything was going to be fine, he thought. He just needed to explain. He had it all worked out. "Let me just explain," he said.

"You sold the shit, yes?" Aldo said.

Sean scooted an inch back. "Yeah, but..."

"And you put all of my money in that pouch of yours, yes?"

Sean felt the sludge in his mouth from so many cigarettes and so little water.

"Yeah, but..."

Aldo looked at Sean. "Which you lost in this fight," he said. His eyes were as soft as ever, as pleasant as ever to behold, but his mouth was drawn tight, his lips thin.

"You look tired, Aldo," Sean said.

"I am tired, Sean." Aldo dropped his leg and then his arms and leaned forward.

"I'll have the money on Monday," Sean said. He leaned forward too. "All of it."

Aldo inspected the nails of his left hand by turning it over and tapping his thumb against them one by one. "From your friend?" he said.

"Yeah."

Aldo leaned forward. He reached out for the table in front of him. He slipped his fingers beneath its edge and flung it over. It slammed into the banquette. Ashtrays thunked against the wall like wet tennis balls.

Sean had instinctively raised his arm and now he watched Aldo move in front of him from underneath his elbow. Aldo was looking down at his feet, at his shoes, at the big Fuck You he said to the world each and every day for birthing him.

"I'm sorry, Aldo," Sean said. "There wasn't time..."

Aldo put a finger to his lips. "Shhhh," he hissed softly and dropped softly to his knees. He slid himself forward and took Sean's left foot in his hand. He nestled the shoe on his thighs and began to unlace it, drawing the shoestring out and then letting it drop. Three times he did this and then slid the shoe off as Sean watched. There was a time, a long time ago, before Sean's mother's next husbands, before his half-brothers and half-sister came along that Sean could only faultily remember that she held his foot just so, trying to get a shoe on. "Be still," he thinks he remembers her saying. But he couldn't be still. He had to turn and twist and bounce. He had to know what the piece of red plastic on the table tasted like. His mother would get exasperated. They were always going to be late. They were always going to miss something because he wouldn't get his shoes on. More than once she chucked him into the car in just his socks and hurled his shoes after him. "You're father was a pain in the ass to dress to!" she would yell.

Aldo placed the shoe beside him. He peeled a stinking stained sock away from Sean's foot and tossed it over his shoulder. He guided Sean's foot back to the rough carpeted floor and began on the other shoe.

"Who's my daddy?" Sean had asked a hundred times. Sometimes his mother said he was a poet, sometimes she said he was a soldier. Once she said he was dead and another time she said he was a mistake. He was many things but never anything for certain until that day in eighth grade and then he was just a dick.

Aldo placed the other shoe next to its brother and tossed the other sock over his shoulder. He pulled both of Sean's feet onto his lap, holding them there, feeling the pale brown skin. Sean felt tingles and tickles darting from his toes and he felt giggles rising up.

"I didn't know you had a foot fetish, Aldo," he said.

Aldo raised his delicate chin and the heavy dark lids of his eyes. He curled a smile around one side of his face and lifted Sean's feet before him. He bent his head and brushed his lips against Sean's toes then slipped

207

the left big one in his mouth. Sean felt the pull of the vacuum, the succulent slithering of the tongue.

"Damn, Aldo," he sighed. He let himself fall back on the banquette, let his arms flop out and his neck arch as Aldo moved to another toe. "This is an entirely new and joyous sensation." He moved his right hand to his crotch to massage the swelling soldier contained within. Sensation rushed through him like fireflies on a summer's night. "I swear, Aldo, I swear I'll have the money on Monday. I'll bring it by." The sucking and slathering was now interspersed with little nibbles and bites. Sean giggled. Aldo was going to eat him up, he thought. "Raven just has to go to the bank and get it out. She's got the money. I swear. You should see her car. She lives in River Oaks. You should meet my bassist. He's got this monster cock. It's fucking ridiculous."

"What kind of car?"

Sean's eyes opened. His hand stopped moving. He saw red walls, red fabric, and four little dark windows covered by little black curtains to protect the stained glass. He looked down at Aldo who was holding his feet.

"A 1958 Buick Roadmaster," he said.

"Is the car here?" Aldo said.

"Yeah, but…"

Aldo grabbed Sean by the ankles, stood and pulled. Sean felt his happy little world of starlight and fireflies shatter and fail as he crashed to the ash and sugar stained floor.

Aldo stood over him, still holding his legs by the ankle. "I'll keep the car."

"No," Sean said. "I just mean she's got money."

"Fine," Aldo said. "She has money. She has agreed to loan you the money at which point you will supposedly give me the money unless you get mugged or lost or decide to buy another drum kit."

Sean thought of the wreckage at Steele's place. "I do need another drum kit," he shouldn't have said out loud. Aldo spread his legs and stomped him in the nuts. He let Sean's legs go and allowed him the courtesy of curling up into a ball as the bass beats thumped through the walls.

"You act like this is a game." Aldo dropped and crawled over Sean, smoothing back his hair and patting his arms. "This band of yours... you act like you've got something better to do." He hovered over him and drew hot breath from the air between them. He peeled back Sean's head and with the middle finger of his right hand he pulled back Sean's right eyelid while the index finger hovered over the pupil. "You don't. Those college pukes, think they're getting ready for the real world, they don't know shit. I've got twenty fucking VC gangsters trying to get into this

209

place and I got a very serious Colombian friend telling me not to let that happen and you come in here wearing those shoes." He let the lid snap back.

Sean fought to control the combustion of pain in his balls but such a thing is waves and waves and can only be ridden out. "Sorry, Aldo," he wept.

"I know," Aldo said. "So, when you're ready," he wiped a tear from Sean's cheek, "I want you to go with Manny to get your friend and I want you to bring her back here and I will explain to her that she will leave her car with me until I see her at my apartment on Monday with the money at which point she can have her car back and whatever is left of you. Nod if you understand."

Sean understood.

"I need some water!" Raven yelled into Kitten's ear. She couldn't tell if the nod of Kitten's silver plated head indicated acceptance or a reflected the music. "I'm going to get water!" she said again.

Kitten looked up at her. "Okay!" She smiled, draped her arms around Raven's neck and pulled her down, locking on to her lips and groping her mouth about. With a giggle and a turn, she let Raven go and twisted off into the heaving crowd.

Raven threaded her way to Zac, who, even with all the lights and bodies crashing, was easy to spot, leaning against a column near the bar, staring up at the girl dancing in the cage. She'd never let herself get stuffed behind metal bars like that, Raven thought. Never again. When she finally reached him, she put her hand on his chest, stretched up on her tip toes and yelled in his ear.

"How are you doing?"

He dropped his eyes and then his head down to her. He smiled a big dumb smile.

"Good," he said. "Really good."

"Have you seen Sean?" she said.

Zac rubbed his head in the negative. Even smiling, Raven thought, the skin under his eyes drooped in the sad way some dog's eyes do.

"I'm going to get some water!"

"Okay."

"Do you want anything?"

"I'm good." He kissed her on the top of her head, slid his arm around her and squeezed her bones together. He was good. He felt good. He felt tingly and alive and thankful. If James and Tori and Kurt hadn't all ended up in a tangled naked rotting heap for Zac to find as his 18th birthday present, he would not have been right there, right then. He would not have done what he did today. He would not be who he was. He wouldn't have sliced and slashed, picked and poked, punched, pounded, imbibed, ingested, bloodied, fucked, or felt so fine. He'd held a raven by her wings. The angel moved within her cage. He was in heaven. He closed his eyes and let it go.

Raven shook herself out and then slipped through the crowd to the bar and ordered a water. She gave the girl tending bar in a too-tight black leather vest $5 and waved her hand at the change, which the girl quickly stuffed into a plastic jug full of ones and fives and tens and twenties. Raven sipped from her plastic cup. When she swallowed it was as if a rain cloud slipped inside her. She felt it drift, bringing relief to the burning rivers of her blood. She wanted air and made her way to the door that led out to the patio. A shaggy-haired guy she didn't know told her she rocked, she really rocked, the whole show rocked, he'd barely escaped and there were some bands from Seattle coming to town and her band should open for them. She said thank you and told him to talk to Sean about that. He said he would and could he buy her a drink. She curled a strand of hair over her ear. She said she had water and he asked if she wanted something else. She said a vodka tonic would be fine and she'd be outside. He nodded his shaggy head and skipped away. She pushed open the door and stepped out into the patio.

There were no stars near Heaven. The adjacent buildings blotted most of them out, or the orange flavored street lights diffused them. She saw clusters of kids here and there, sitting on black benches, smoking and talking or standing and talking and smoking. She pulled out her cloves and lit one. She held the sweet smoke in her mouth, letting just a tiny bit seep down into her lungs, then exhaled into the heavy air. She liked the way her skin looked in the misty light, and she liked how it felt to be sleek and shiny and do things with a guitar that not many other people could do. She could think of maybe twenty in the whole world. She took a drag of her clove and let the smoke linger. She allowed there might be more.

Some kids she knew called her name and waved her over to one of the benches. She waved back but didn't move. She was happy with herself. She could feel the music thumping through the walls. She could feel the night. She thought she could see a song in the smoke lifting away from her fingers.

"Raven, hey," a soft voice said. She felt his hand on the small of her back and smiled. She closed her eyes and turned.

She opened her eyes. It wasn't the shaggy haired boy. It was Sean. He was looking up at her. "Thank you for tonight," she said to him and wrapped him in her long arms. She nestled her face in his neck and kissed his cheek. He held her too but held her back at the same time.

"Yeah," he said.

She frowned and pulled back. It was hard to tell if he was looking at her because he was wearing her very best, very dark sunglasses and there was a crack in the right lens that wasn't there when they came in.

"Raven," he said.

"What's wrong?" she said.

He smiled even wider. His hand had moved from her back to her arm.

"Nothing," he said. "Aldo needs to talk to you."

Raven took a step back.

"It's nothing," he said. "He just wants to talk to you."

She pulled at her clove.

"Why does he want to talk to me?"

Sean looked over at a cluster of kids by the wall.

"It's stupid," Sean said. He took his hair out of the pony tail, flipped it out and then twisted it back in. He snapped a quick glance at the giant of a man standing against the wall looking off and away. He was the biggest man she'd ever seen and she'd just sacrificed her virginity upon a very big man. He wore all black. He had mirrored sunglasses. A massive silver cross rested on his expansive chest. His head moved like a granite block sliding over a greased floor. He was looking at her.

"Is that Aldo?"

214

Sean smiled. "No, that's just Manny. He's a pussycat. He'll take us to Aldo. It's nothing. It's so stupid. He just wants us to promise. He's weird like that." He took her elbow and turned her back to the door. "Come on," he said. "It will only take a second."

Raven pulled her arm away. "I don't like this," she said.

"Raven," Sean said. "I just need to show him that you're a real person and that you really are going to lend me the money and he really will get paid and then we can go and dance the night away."

Sean looked small and silly with his long hair in a ponytail, dark sunglasses, pink t-shirt, red pants and bare feet. He came towards her and put his hands on her arms.

"What happened to your shoes?"

Sean shrugged. "I took them off. It will only take a second," he said. He moved his hands up, along her neck and then into her white hair. She felt his touch like electric shocks. It made her teeth hurt. She wanted him fiercely and she couldn't say why except that he was like an ice cream sundae.

"Okay," she said. She dropped the clove onto the cement tile and crushed it out with her boot. Sean took Raven's hand in his and led her back inside. Manny held open the door for them.

2.

Kitten thought she was full and enough was enough and dancing it out would be enough. But she wasn't. She wanted more. She wanted to devour everyone, lap them all up like milk and cough them all out later. But she couldn't eat everyone so just one would have to do.

She wriggled her way free of the hands that were holding her and slithered out of the crowd. He was two pillars away. She ducked and danced and then stood before him, looking up, way up and then she looked straight forward and laughed. She didn't even come up to his chest. She was just about to grab him in the privates and give him a goose when she saw Sean leading Raven past the bar and leapt out at them.

She gave Sean a quick kiss on the cheek, embraced Raven and nuzzled to her ear. "Can I have the keys to the car, please?" she purred.

"What for?" Raven said.

"I need to talk to Clair," she said and laughed.

Raven giggled and dug in her bag for her keys. She slipped them into Kitten's. "Do NOT drive it and try NOT to stain the seat!"

"Okay!" Kitten said, gave her a wet kiss on the cheek and danced back to Zac. She grabbed his ass giving it a good, hard squeeze which made him jump and drop his cup of melted ice. The water splashed on his legs and the shoulder of a boy just in front of him.

The boy turned around to say something but didn't.

"Sorry!" Zac said.

"S'cool," the boy said. "Y'all rocked tonight!"

"Thanks," Zac said. He stared down at the cup and then turned and saw Kitten. "Hi!" he said.

"Hi." She took his arm in both of hers and tugged. She nibbled at her lip as she led him away from the dancing, twisting, swirling, rubbing, grinding, flowing, ebbing, stripping, squeezing mass and towards the exit door. He looked back, up at the angel moving her body slowly in the cage.

Sean wanted to get this over with. He would just have to convince her it would be okay. He just needed to get Aldo paid off and then he would be done with all of it. He'd dedicate himself to the band. He'd go to Sound Engineering School. It would all be fine and dandy and good if he could just get Raven to go along with it and convince Aldo to let him keep his eyes.

He pulled at Raven again.

217

"What?" she said.

"Just in here," he said to her and pulled her through the black door on the far wall.

"Stop dragging me!" She wrenched her arm free of his grip and stopped just inside the door.

"Come on," he said.

"Sean?" she said.

He turned and looked at her. Add ten pounds to her and she could still win Miss Texas Teen Gothic Princess of Darkness, he thought.

"What?" he said.

"What is going on?' she said quietly.

"Nothing," he said. "We just need to leave Aldo your car."

Sean felt that he had said it the nicest way possible. He was reasonably sure that coming out and saying it like that would be best because at least she would know that he didn't try to trick her and he'd have a chance to explain before they went in to see Aldo.

Kitten led Zac out front exit, past the wraith sitting on his stool and the small line of kids waiting to get in, up the cracked stone steps and across the street to the big black car. She fussed with the keys and then opened the back seat door. She crawled in and when Zac hesitated, she reached out and dragged him in by the belt.

218

She started to undo her boots.

"What are we doing?" he asked.

"What do you think we're doing?" she said. She'd double knotted and the gloves were making her fingers slip so she tore off the gloves and tore at the laces.

"I don't know," he said. He sat back and looked out the window. He saw the club and Manny and the kids waiting, doing little spin moves and making nervous jokes. The cracked buildings stood like ancient totems along a dark road snuggled by weed filled lots. A cluster of kids huddled under a sagging awning just down the street.

Kitten got the first boot off and started on the second.

"All I need to you do, Zac," she said, "is shut up and fuck me."

"Is that all?"

Kitten stopped. She looked over at Zac. He looked like the big, sad teddy bear she used to whisper stained secrets to. The one she ripped the stuffing out of and burned in the back yard.

"Stop being a fag," she said.

Zac took a shallow breath and heaved it out. "Maybe I am a fag," he said. It was the thing most dreaded by the football, baseball and basketball players he'd grown up with. It was the thing most feared by their fathers and coaches, acts they told him never to do. If they hobbled over to the sideline they were told to walk it off and stop acting like a sissy. If they

219

stopped to smell a flower, they were called a girl. James had said it was all bullshit, that half of the dads were cruising Pacific Street on Wednesday nights.

Kitten got the other boot off.

"You're not a fag."

"I let a guy suck my dick."

She peeled off her tights and panties, hiked up her skirt and lay back on the wide red seat.

"That was just Sean," she said. She slapped at her pussy and rubbed the piercing through her clit. "Let's go."

Zac looked over at her. Kitten's face was slashed by a shadow. Her eyes bore into him. Her lips were parted, her teeth set. Her scarred and charred arms reached out for him. Her legs were spread and between them it sparkled.

"I am not giving him my car!" Raven said.

Sean flapped his arms. "It's only until Monday!" he said.

Raven arced a finger at him. "Sean," she said. "I worked too hard for that car." She'd seen the car at the Antique and Unique Auto Dealership just before she'd turned eighteen and made her friend pull over so she could circle it, see her reflection in its sleek black sides. In that reflection she was neither skinny nor pale but a dark being of immeasurable power. She'd walked across too many stages in too little clothing. She'd worn too many smiles and waved in too many parades. She'd stood motionless for hours when every nerve within screamed out to shred. She had to sue her mother for access to her prize monies to buy it. "No one gets my car!"

Sean stepped close to her. "He's going to rip out one of my eyes," he pleaded.

"Then you can keep the sunglasses," Raven said.

Sean jumped back and stomped down. His hands balled up into fists which he shook in the air. "Why doesn't anyone just fucking do this shit!"

The far door opened and Aldo stepped into the hallway just as the door to the club opened behind them and Manny came in and closed the door, forcing Raven and Sean forward towards Aldo. The office opened and the balding man stuck his goggle-eyed head out.

"Hey," he said.

"Mind your business, Phil," Aldo said.

Phil's head disappeared and the door snapped shut.

Aldo stepped back from the entrance to the small lounge. He gestured with his arm for them to kindly enter.

"Come on, Raven," Sean said. He took her hand, hung his head and pulled her gently towards Aldo and the open door.

"I don't have the keys," she said.

221

Sean turned. "What?"

"I don't have the keys. I gave them to Kitten." She looked from Sean to Aldo. He looked like an angel that had not quite fallen all the way down to hell. "I have to go get the car keys," she said to him.

Aldo's eyes shifted from Raven to Sean and then back. "Where is Kitten?" he said.

"Out in the car," Raven replied. She wrapped her arms around herself. She started to shiver.

Aldo gestured to the delivery door. "This door will take you out. You will come back to it and knock twice." He knocked on the wall, once and then paused and then again. "Manny will go with you," he said and stepped aside.

Raven moved towards the door but it seemed a hundred feet away and Aldo stopped her half-way there with a hand to her chest. It felt so warm. "I understand there is a gun," Aldo said to Manny. "Bring that as well."

"Say my name," Kitten hissed in Zac's ear.

"Why?"

"Just say it," she said. "Say it over and over."

She clawed at his hips, trying to push him faster and deeper inside her. She wanted all of him and more of him. As much as there was to him

222

it wasn't enough. She needed to hear her name. She needed to know it was her that he wanted, that it was her that he was fucking. All those doctors, all those years, they got it all so very wrong.

"Kitten."

"Say it like you mean it!"

"Kitten."

"Yes, daddy!" she sighed and gasped as Zac sassquashed his whole self at her unable to deny the pleasures of a form fitting sheath.

"Kitten, Kitten, Kitten."

"Here is Edward Bear," she hissed. "Coming down the stairs now, bump, bump bump…"

Zac heard her from sometime long ago.

"Bump, bump bump on the back of his head," she panted. "It's… it's the only way of coming downstairs."

They were playing goblin, ghost and witch when he fell down the stair and hit his head. A bleeding gash opened over his eye. His sister held him in her arms as his brother looked for the bandages. They wrapped him up in a towel and almost half a roll of tape. They told him he was King Tut and they laughed and laughed until his mother came home and gave him stitches.

"Don't stop. Why are you stopping?" she said. She tried to pull him and push him but he was too big to move. "Where are you going?"

Zac tried to withdraw. "I don't know."

"I'll hold you tight, I won't ever let go." Kitten pulled at him, wrapped her legs around him, squeezed him tight within her, bent forward and dotted sweet kisses and affectionate nips at his nipples.

"Stop it," he said.

"No!"

She dug her claws into his flesh. He screamed and as he screamed he arched his back and thrust so deep inside her she felt like she might split. This was him fucking her. This was him inside. She cried for more and he gave it to her. He punished her and she loved it. She felt it coming like a tidal wave, drawing away, the build, the build and then the crash that washes mountains away. She saw lightning flash and felt heat splitting the air as the back window of the Buick shattered and a million tiny shards of glass tore through the air, slicing and imbedding as Zac screamed and Kitten came.

Raven felt the velvet cord connection between her and Aldo snap as their skin parted and Manny moved her towards the door. She looked back but only saw the last flip of Sean's pony-tail as he was led into a room. Manny put a hand on the small of her back, reached over her shoulder and shoved the Fire Exit open. Raven gasped.

There was a kid in sunglasses, sleek dark hair, wearing a black suit standing on the other side. Behind him Raven could see several more kids in black suits with white shirts and black ties. They all looked like Sean and they all had knives except for the one with the gas can.

The hand in her back shoved her forward and then the kid at the door shoved her down. There were shouts and leather-soled feet pounding past her. One of them stomped on her calf. Another kicked her in the head.

"Yes! Yes!" Kitten howled.

"God damn it!" Zac bellowed.

"Don't stop! Don't stop!"

"Someone just shot at us!" Zac yelled. He shoved himself off of her and moved to pull his shorts back up but in so doing sat on the little chunks of glass and screamed. He pressed his shoulders against the seat back and his feet into the floor boards and arched up, Claire glistening in the swampy light, wiping with his hands across his ass to get the glass off.

Kitten sat up. She looked out of the empty space where the back window used to be. Three small figures burst from the weeded lot next to them, slithered between the parked cars, and dashed across the street towards the club where they met up with the pack that had been waiting under the awning. She saw the kids who had been waiting to get in

225

scattering, running this way and that. She saw St. Peter sprawled motionless in front of the door as Heaven fell.

Sean and Aldo turned to see Manny crash to the floor, clutching at a kid in a suit who was stabbing him in the chest over and over and over. Then there were more of them, an ancient dragon spitting fire and flashing talons. Two of them piled onto Manny, trying to slay the giant and save their friend. Three more of them rushed into the room.

Sean scurried to the banquet. He saw Aldo crumple and thrash and heard the snicks of three blades entering and exiting his body. The assassins grunted with the work and when they were done they stood. One of them spat on Aldo's torn face. Another one kicked the twitching leg. The last one looked at Sean.

Sean held up his hands.

The guy's white shirt was stained red and slick wet splotches covered his suit and tie. He held up his right hand. There was a dark slice across the palm. He said something in Vietnamese and pointed at Aldo. The other two laughed. Sean laughed too. The kid with the gas can came panting to the door. He yelled. The guy in front of Sean spit and swore. He barked commands to his friends and they rushed out. The guy turned, pointed at Aldo again, said something else to Sean and followed the others out turning towards the door that led to the club. Sean heard them run down the hall. He heard the club door open and the music pound. He looked down at Aldo.

Aldo's fine white suit had been shredded into rags of pink and red. Sean took his sunglasses off.

Aldo's mouth was moving. He was trying to say something.

Sean lowered himself to the carpet and nestled his head beside Aldo's. They looked into each other's eyes. Aldo's deep brown pupils contracted and released, shuttered from left to right and back again.

"Help..."

Sean's eyes were a fading storm on a desert plain. He bent forward and kissed Aldo on the forehead.

"I'm sorry, Frank," he whispered in his ear.

Sean sat back up. Aldo's eyes were dead, blank pools going cold. He rummaged through Aldo's pants, pulled out the swollen money clip and stuffed it into his pocket.

Sean picked up his shoes and walked out of the room. The music had stopped. He could hear screams and firecrackers going off. Manny lay in a heap. One of the boys in his black suit lay next to him, his head at an unnatural angle to his body.

Phil's head popped out of the office door, saw Sean and popped back in.

Sean turned to the Fire Exit and found Raven trying to get to her feet just outside.

"You okay?" He took her by the waist and helped her up.

"I think so," she said. There was dirt on the side of her face and a red inked stain in her white hair. "I can walk." She shoved Sean away and started to stagger in the wrong direction.

Sean took hold of her again and guided her around to the alley that would take them back to her car. "Come on, baby," he said. "We gots to bowl before these guys figure out I ain't all VC."

Zac and Kitten watched as Heaven burned. Black smoke poured from the windows and doors as the club disgorged its inhabitants. The cherubs and the demons clawed and fought their way out of the gates. They climbed the garden fences and broke open the stained windows, leaving their drinks and drugs, their friends and blood behind.

"There!" said Kitten.

A lumbering form, like a three legged dog, staggered across the street. Raven's boots smacked on the asphalt as Sean pulled her to the car.

"Keys!" Raven shouted.

"Start the fucking car!" Sean screamed.

Kitten dove down to the floorboards and hunted among the shards of glass for Raven's keys. She found them under her tights and held them

228

out as Raven came to the driver's side door and Sean slid around to the passenger's side.

"Open the door!" Raven cried.

Zac bent forward and pulled up the lock. Raven snatched the door open, sat, grabbed the keys and shoved them into the ignition.

"Hey!" Sean shouted.

Raven turned the key, gunned the gas and the Buick roared to life.

"Door!" Sean screamed. Kitten pulled herself forward with the back of the seat and pulled up the lock. Sean wrenched the door open and just managed to climb in as Raven turned and backed up, then shifted to forward, turned again, then into reverse, cranking the wheel.

"Go," Sean said. "You have to go!"

Four young men in black suits and white shirts were racing around the building, scouring the street, pointing up and down.

Raven saw them and her foot slipped. She cracked into the car behind her and swore. She snapped the shift into drive and bashed her way out, knocking the compact in front of her three feet down the street into a pick-up. The young men ran towards them but the Buick had its nose to the wind and tore down the road with a snarl.

Looking back, Zac saw the angel stumble into the street, fighting to tear off her burning wings with the arm not hanging loosely from its socket.

Spinning lights of red and blue rushed toward them. Sirens called. The angel looked to the beer colored sky before she fell to the black tar street.

3.

"The cops are going to want to talk to me, aren't they?" Sean said.

No one answered. The wind sang through the open windows, whipping their hair and flapping at their skin.

He had told them, in a slow, measured voice, what had happened in the club, the threats, the car, the VC busting in and Aldo dying. He didn't mention the money he'd taken from Aldo's pocket. Looking Vietnamese had saved him but now he was afraid he'd be lumped in with them. The cops would start asking who Aldo was with, and there were only about a hundred people at the club who would tell them. If they thought he'd been working with the VC, he'd go to jail. If the VC ever figured out who he really was, he'd probably end up dead. In that moment, Sean realized his days of surfing delightedly through downtown clubs was over. His eyes drifted, his mouth drooped.

After Zac explained the gunshot through the back glass, Raven threatened to turn the car around and pull a drive by. It was an empty threat.

She didn't need Sean and Zac to tell her what a bad idea it was. She told them both to shut the fuck up. She drove angry. She gunned the Buick out of the warehouse district, empty streets flashing by while sirens faded. She roared up the ramp on to I-10 East. The night was waning thin and at this hour, there were very few cars. The Buick growled alone along a concrete river. She could have kept going, all the way to the Atlantic Ocean, but Raven directed it south instead when they reached the 610 loop, for no reason other than that south was where birds fled when the cold winds blew and played a nighttime dirge.

Kitten peered just above the edge of the open window, pulling deep on a cigarette. She felt nuggets of glass embedding in her naked legs and treasured every one. The spires of downtown twinkled in the distance as the road dipped and rose. She hadn't gone outside the thirty mile wide loop in almost three years. She thought about the astronauts. She'd met a girl in group whose father had blown up and fell down as ash. She thought about the astronauts and how frightening it must be, to be so high above the world, to see it spinning down below their feet, not sure they'd ever return.

"Take 225 South," Zac said.

He didn't know if Raven heard him, so he carefully pulled himself forward. He thought he had swept most of the glass onto the floorboards but every time he shifted, he seemed to find a new translucent cube biting into his butt.

"Take 225," he said louder.

"Why?" Raven said.

"I have a beach house in Kemah." He looked over at Sean and then back to Raven. "We can crash there."

Sean was looking at his hands. "Is anyone there?" he said.

"No." Zac sat back, finding two more pieces of glass with his butt. His jaw hurt from smiling so much and his back was sore. He could feel his face puffing up and his ribs clutching at his breath. The happiness, the utter joy of life he had experienced an hour before, was wearing off, thinning out. His head throbbed and his eyes felt like lights that had been left on too long.

Kitten curled up in the corner. She slipped on her gloves. She didn't mind the glass, or the cuts but she cursed the chill from the wind. She tossed her cigarette out the empty space behind her, watched it burst like a tiny firecracker and snuggled into the pocket of warmth she'd found near the rear speaker. The music washed over her and she was fascinated by the feel of the leather seat with so many shiny sharp pebbles upon it.

Raven took the long swooping curve that carried them further south on the Pasadena Highway. The rotten smell of refineries hit them from the east before they could properly see the thousands and thousands of lights that dotted and danced over the acres and acres of pipes, smokestacks, storage containers and oil tankers.

The freeway ended but the road went on. To the east, the refineries belched greasy fumes, while in the darkness to the west, rows of dilapidating houses and crusting mobile homes slept. There were few buildings along this stretch, no malls or big box stores. The road began to slowly slip away from the twisted metal constructions. Then it ended at a t-intersection.

"Which way," Raven said.

Zac sat up. He'd been thinking about what he usually thought about, and about going back to the place where all those thoughts began. He didn't want to. He didn't want to go there or think about there or think about going there but felt, or wanted to feel, or constructed the feelings that allowed him to believe that he must.

"Right," he said. "Keep going south until after the big bridge."

Raven waited for a tanker truck to rumble by and turned right.

They drove. More refineries rose up from the swampy land as Raven stared at the road with dragging eyes and Sean stared at his hand. Zac drank in the smells and watched the flames dance on the burn towers. Kitten curled further into her corner.

The refineries gave way to fishing shacks and boat slips as they came to the bridge that spanned Clear Lake's mouth to the sea. From high above, they could see the moonlight dancing on the water but the smell of an ocean was still missing as they drifted down the other side where Kemah squatted dull and dark, the three restaurants and the ice cream place that constituted its boardwalk closed hours ago.

"Left at the light," Zac said and Raven slowed as she approached the blinking yellow. She put on her turn signal and nosed the Buick to the left but she was not prepared for the way the road kept curving away and down and scutted halfway off into the gravel and almost into a ditch before steering back on course.

Sean had stopped staring at his hands because he needed to grab hold of something. Kitten got smushed in the corner.

"Shit!" Raven said.

"Sorry," Zac said. "I should have warned you about that."

"You think?" Raven straightened the car out.

"Sorry," Zac said. He pointed over her shoulder at a small green sign. "Right here. Then just a couple blocks," he said and then sat back again.

"Fuck," Raven said and then she said it again because red and blue lights erupted behind her and a siren whooped.

Sean's head whipped around and then back. "Fuck me," he said. "Game over, man! Game over."

"What is it?" Kitten stammered.

Zac put his hand on her thigh.

"It's okay," he said.

"Go! Just go!" Sean felt hydrogen smashing in his chest. He wanted to run, he wanted to fly. Raven had slowed to a crawl but she hadn't stopped all the way. A sharp light was blinding them from behind. "Drive you stupid skinny bitch!"

Raven slammed her foot on the brake.

Kitten's eyes turned wild. "Nonononononononoooo...."

Zac put his other hand on Raven's shoulder. "It's okay."

Sean cranked his head into his chest, shielding it from the light. "This is not okay!"

Raven punched at him.

"Fuck you, you fucking junkie fuck!"

"NONONONONO!"

"Stupid skinny bitch!"

Zac heaved himself forward, thrust Sean one way and Raven the other and held them there. "Calm down," he said. "It's okay. I'll know them."

A slash of light cut across Sean's blue eyes gone ghost white. "You'll know them?"

"I hope so," he said. He turned to Raven. "Get the license and registration, just in case." Then he turned back to Sean. "Chill."

Sean nodded.

Zac released them and sank back into the back seat. He looked down at Kitten.

"Look at me, baby," he said.

Kitten looked up. "Nonono," she said.

"It's going to okay, okay? I'm here."

"Daddy's here?" Kitten looked up. She looked like a little baby girl whose older brother had abused her with a stapler.

"Daddy will take care of it," Zac said. "Okay?"

Kitten knew that Daddy always took care of it. He always bandaged her up afterwards and the fear melted away from her. Her hands released her arms and the skin started to smooth out as the blood returned. "Okay," she said.

Zac gave her one more squeeze on her leg. He rolled back gingerly, opened his door and stepped out. He shut the door and disappeared into the light.

Raven watched him in the mirror until she couldn't see him anymore. She glanced at Sean. "Hand me the little book in the glove compartment," she said to him.

Sean snapped to life. He twisted the knob and pulled down the little door. He took out the little book and handed it to Raven.

"You're too good," he said.

"What?"

She put the book next to her. He put his hand on hers.

"I never tried to have sex with you because you're too good. I want you to know that. Your talent is vicious. It'll swallow us all up. But listen," he glanced back at the lights then back to her, "...no matter what happens, if we all go off to prison or something, do not stop playing."

Her head hurt. She didn't look at Sean. She wouldn't, because then she might believe him. She pulled her hand out from under his and dug in her bag for her purse and then dug in her purse for her license. She looked down at the license at a girl with blond hair and brown roots, smiling ever so perfectly into the camera. It was a nice picture of a girl she didn't know anymore. Some girl named Karen who could always stand to lose five pounds according to her mother. Raven looked at the long thin claw that held the card. Why, her mother had asked her so many times, wouldn't she eat after she stopped competing? Why, when her mother had to rip the bag of cheese chips away from her an hour before swimsuits, wouldn't she have some brisket at her cousins wedding? And why did she have to ruin her hair and dress like death warmed over all the time and it was all her father's fault for teaching her guitar and learning her how to shoot a gun and running around with whores all the time!

She remembered the day her dad told her that lawyers could rock out too was the day she changed her name.

A blinding light approached from the rear, it moved to the passenger side.

"Did I ever tell y'all about the time I stole home plate?" Sean said.

"No," Raven said.

His chin tucked to his chest, Sean slid his right hand as slowly and easily as he could into his pants pocket. He grasped the smooth metal bend of the money clip and then tried to get the knife in his fingertips as well. The light illuminated the missing window and searched along the shattered glass-covered seat.

"It was in little league, in the All-Star game. We were playing this team from Memorial. It was the last game because we were already mathematically eliminated from going on to the regional's," he said. He had both the knife and money pinned between two fingers but couldn't get them out. He let the clip go and clasped the knife. "So it didn't matter. The game didn't matter. I got a single and then, this kid, Eric, got a hit and I made it to third. I think there was one out." He slid the knife out, millimeters at a time until he got it into his hand and pressed it against his leg. "And Refugio, our big hitter, we used to call him Lard Ass. He was a big kid and really dark so he had to play Chewbacca every time we played Star Wars at the playground. He really wanted to be Han Solo but I was always Han Solo."

The light moved to the front as Sean shoved the knife into the fold of the seat and pressed it down. Raven saw him in silhouette. She watched his mouth move.

"So I'm on third and Lard Ass comes up and the coach for the other team tells the pitcher to intentionally walk him so they can get a double play or something. It was just dumb because this is our last little league game, you know. The score doesn't matter. Just let the kid pitch and let Lard Ass hit," Sean said. The light moved to the front of the car and lingered there, lighting up both their faces. Sean reached back into his pocket for the money. "The pitcher seemed to think the same way and was really pissed about it so after he threw the first pitch way, way outside, he waited for the ball and when he got it he hung his head and slouched back to the mound and I'm standing on third thinking, 'I can steal home!'" He got the money clip out of his pocket and slid it, too, into the fold of the seat. The light moved to Raven's side.

"So I tag up," Sean said. "And the next pitch, I sort of test how far I can go down the baseline."

Kitten saw the handle of the knife sliding through the front seat. She watched it drop and fall to the glass covered floor. She could hear voices out the back window but couldn't catch the words. She was down in the dark listening to Sean talking about stealing a house.

240

"Kid throws a ball. Catcher just tosses it back and turns around to go back to his spot. The pitcher gets the ball and trudges back up the mound and I'm, like, half-way to home plate and no one's noticed so I go tag up again and wait, and start inching towards home. The pitcher throws another ball and as soon as the catcher starts to toss it back I take off! I'm watching the pitcher and he just catches it and turns around."

Raven couldn't help from blinking as the light hovered next to her face. She saw the outline of a dark uniform and the glint of metal rings hanging from a belt.

"So, I'm running," Sean said. "And the first person to see what I'm doing is my coach and he starts yelling, 'Sean! What the fuck are you doing! GO! GO! GO!' And then the crowd on our side starts yelling and then the crowd on their side starts yelling and then the other coach starts yelling and the catcher is yelling and finally the pitcher looks up and sees I'm about a foot from the plate and he hurls the ball way over the catcher's head and I'm safe."

The light went out. Footsteps crunched away.

Sean looked up. "So that's the time I stole home."

"Did you win the game?" Raven said.

He looked over at her. "You know, I think we did," he said.

The thought occurred to Kitten that even though the light had gone out and Sean had saved his house, something could still go horribly wrong

241

and she ought to have the knife. She leaned forward and reached out, touching the handle with trembling fingers. She pulled it towards her, scraping it along the glassy expanse until she could get a proper grip on it and pull it to her chest. She cradled it there and waited.

Raven, Sean and Kitten waited.

The blinding light behind them cut off. The red and blue ones swirled down.

The back door cranked open. Zac reached in and brushed more of the glass off the seat. He got in.

"It's okay," he said. "One more block and then a right and then the second driveway on your left."

Sean turned around. "What did you say?"

"I said we were at a show at the Palladium and some skinheads put a brick through the window and we got into it with them a little bit but everything's cool now. Nothing to report," Zac said. "Go ahead, Raven." He put his hand back on Kitten's thigh and gave her a pat-pat.

Raven put the Buick in gear and rolled slowly forward.

"They believed that?" Sean said.

"They know me."

"Why do they know you?"

Raven put on her blinker and turned right onto Bay Street.

"Because," Zac said, leaning forward and pointing to the second mailbox, a battered and rusted blue one next to a For Sale sign, "this is where my brother and his girlfriend and his best friend all died. Turn here."

Kitten sat up to look as Raven came to a stop.

"Is it...?" she said.

Zac felt an adrenaline shot in his throat but touched her lightly on the shoulder. "It's fine. It was all cleaned up. There's this service which specializes in that sort of thing."

"Fun job," Sean said.

Raven turned the car, inching over the gravel in the drive that curled through hanging branches and whispering grass. The lights cutting through the foliage revealed patches of a squat, light blue shack. She brought the battered car to a stop, turned off the ignition and as the music faded, they could hear waves and smell the salt sea air.

4.

"So that's the ocean," Zac said.

Sean, Raven and Kitten looked beyond a small clipped yard and

over a low wall at the dark expanse, highlighted by moonlight and defined

by the red and blue and orange lights of the oil rigs hunched just over the

dark horizon and the tankers moving towards the Houston Ship Channel and

the refineries across the water.

Zac turned and lifted an egg-shaped rock. He picked up the silver

key hidden beneath it, dropped the rock back into place and stood. Raven

pulled at her clove and stared out over the Gulf of Mexico as it wavered in

the moonlight. Sean gaped at the blinking lights. Kitten swayed in the

darkness, feeling the knife she had slipped into her right glove, and looked

down at her bare, bloody feet.

Zac pulled open the screen door and inserted the key into the

polished new lock set into the weathered old boards. "My dad bought this place fifteen years ago." He turned the key and the lock clicked. He pushed in the door. "We got to use it for a like a year before he rented it out." It smelled of musty heat and the sea. Zac slipped the key into his pocket and stepped inside. The screen door slammed behind him. He snapped on the front light. Nothing moved or stirred except the sweat that began to pour from his skin.

He turned and cranked open the windows.

"When he was 21, James took over the lease. He said he would pay my dad rent but I don't know if he ever did. He and Kurt moved in and mostly smoked pot, played D&D and started a new band."

Raven pulled open the screen door, stepped inside and let it slam shut. Four plain wooden chairs surrounded a small table to her left. There was a wicker couch and wicker coffee table to the right, set to look out on the sea. She watched Zac move to the kitchen, unlatch a window and shove it up. He moved past a thin set of stairs and went down a short dark hallway. She saw him pop on a light and step inside a bare white bathroom. He shut the door. With the windows open, the salty air blew through and dust shifted on the tables. Raven could feel the emptiness of it. She thought she heard it sigh.

There was a flush and the bathroom door opened. Zac came out. He turned to his left and went into a room. A moment later he came out.

He took a step towards the door across from where he stood but stopped. His hand lifted and then fell. He came back down the hall towards Raven.

"James met Tori at the boardwalk. Tori worked at the ice-cream stand down there. She was just this stupid girl but he used to go down there with his boom-box blasting Beethoven and draw pictures of her 50's pin-up style. Drove her crazy, I guess. Drove the cops crazy too because you can't really bust a kid for playing Beethoven and drawing cute pictures some of the tourists would buy, even if he does have a giant purple Mohawk. I used to have a painting of her that he did. Do you want some water?"

At the suggestion, Raven felt how dry her throat was. "Yes," she said.

Zac went to the cupboard and took out a glass, then he went to the sink. "She was a junior in high school like me. Pretty soon she was over all the time." He washed the glass and then filled it. He tested it and then filled it again and handed it to Raven. "My mom comes out sometimes and dusts. I think my dad stays here sometimes. I don't know."

Raven took the glass from him. She took a sip. It tasted a little swampy but it was cool. She felt like a limp noodle that had been tossed against a wall and left to slowly sink and slide and, finally, peel and fall to the dusty floor. The water helped.

Sean came in. The screen door smacked behind him.

"Water?" Zac said to Sean.

246

"Yeah," Sean said. He sat down on the couch. A small cloud of dust lifted into the thick air.

Zac retrieved a glass. "I came over here on the day of my 18th birthday. James was going to throw a party for me." He washed and filled the glass and took it to Sean. "I came in and the place smelled like rotting meat, even though all the windows were open." Zac turned and looked down the hallway. "You can't really smell it anymore. They did a good job of cleaning it up."

Sean held the glass of water, looked at it and kept holding it.

Zac edged his way down the hall.

"I found them in..." he pointed to the door he hadn't gone in. "They were all naked and there was blood everywhere. It soaked into the rugs. There were brains on the walls..."

"Jesus..." Raven said.

Zac stopped. "Sorry." He pulled the key out of his pocket.

Sean stared at the glass and the water and saw blood oozing out of slices in his skin.

"There's another bedroom and two twin beds up in the loft." Zac wandered to the base of the steps. "I hit my head here once. Bandaged up like a mummy." He turned to the hall. "Bathroom's back there." Raven watched him sit down on the floor. He pressed the tip of the key into the boards with his black painted fingers and drew it toward him. A little curl of wood trailed the key.

"We were playing this dungeon one time," he said. "It was this messed up dungeon that James had just made up. It didn't make any sense. You went in one room and there was a dragon, and in the next room there would be, like, a hundred gnomes dancing naked, and we had this pack mule that eventually got eaten by a troll, I think." He dug at the wood with the key. "We were in this passage and there was a ten foot pit in the middle of it, and we couldn't figure out how to get the pack mule across. James said all you needed to get a pack mule across a ten foot pit was 50' of rope and a battle-axe." Zac placed the key on its side and slid it back and forth across the floor. "He was on top." He looked up at Sean. "He was the last one to fall." He turned his head to Raven. "Do you understand? How do you do that and not tell your kid brother how the fuck to get a pack mule across a ten foot pit with a battle axe and 50' of rope?"

Raven put her glass down on the table and knelt beside him. She rubbed her hand over his back as he pressed his head to the floor and clutched at his hair. "Shhhh," she said. "Shhhh."

"Dude," Sean said. He wanted to mention something to Zac but was afraid to talk. He wanted to say something clever, something positive, something funny or witty or wise but he was all used up. He felt like the deflated balloon waiting for another cylinder of nitrous. Then he saw the frog sitting by the front door.

"Zac!"

Zac looked up. His brown eyes rimmed red, shot by crimson veins, his face slick with dirt streaked, his Mohawk collapsed into sticky strands. Sean was pointing. He was pointing at a frog just inside the door.

"The frog," Sean said.

"From your dream," Raven said. "When your brother came to visit you and left you a bag full of frogs."

"Dude," Sean said. "He's here."

Zac edged forward on his hands and knees.

The frog sat blinking and glistening in the warm light. Its throat billowed and collapsed. Its wide dark eyes blinked back and forth.

Zac crawled as close as he dared. He reached out his hand, laying out his open palm.

The frog blinked.

Raven stood. She bit her lip. It wasn't a frog. It was a toad.

"Don't pick it up…," she warned.

Zac swept up the frog up and lifted him to his face.

The toad released a warm gush of piss in Zac's hand then hopped out one of the open windows.

"…or that will happen," Raven said to herself.

249

Zac rose to his knees. He could hear locusts and waves.

"What do you think he was trying to tell me?"

"I don't know, man." Sean put the glass down on the coffee table. He rolled off the wicker couch, onto his knees and scooted next to Zac. "Maybe just," he looped a thin brown arm over the big man's shoulder, "that you have to let him go."

Raven stepped forward. "Or he'll pee on you."

Zac looked at his hand. He laughed. He looked up at Raven. "Get over this shit or I'll pee on your head. That's so him." He laughed again. He laughed like a man gone mad or one who has suddenly been released from long confinement or one who thought he had long been confined and gone mad and suddenly realized it was just a Tuesday.

Sean chuckled slightly, gave the big guy a squeeze and pushed himself back up on the couch. Raven drifted back to the kitchen to light a clove.

"What a crazy fucking day," Zac said.

Sean slapped his hands on his legs. The shot of pain reminded him that one of his hands had gotten sliced pretty good. He looked down at it. The superglue still held. He looked back up at Zac.

"My mom used to ask us, me and my step-brothers, when we had dinner together, what the best part of our day was," Sean said. "It got really annoying when I got to be a teenager. She tried, I guess."

Raven thought about her sacrifice and she thought about the cheesecake. She thought about the look on the shaggy haired boy's face and Kitten's gyrations on the dance floor. "Playing," she said. "When we were playing."

"That was mine too," Sean said although he had to admit the toe-sucking thing was up there.

"Me too," Zac said.

"I know, right?" Sean squealed. "When Kitten came running up and goes, "We're Double Murder Suicide and this is Fuck Me Open" we just took off!" He did a little air-guitar move. "That was sweet."

Raven slouched back. She followed every note, every bridge and every fill right up to the point where Steele came crashing in. "Those poor fish," she said.

"Dude, we trashed that fucking place." Sean's toes started tapping. "Then we blew up Heaven!"

"Don't forget the orgy," Raven said.

Sean leapt up and danced over to her. He pulled her to him, twisted her round and dipped her. "How could I forget?" he said.

"Wait till we go on tour," Zac said.

Sean jumped up. Lifting his hands to the sky he exclaimed, "We are going to unleash the ancient fires! Fuck hotel rooms. We are going to trash the planet!" He flapped his legs in a spastic sort of chicken dance type of a thing.

Then he stopped and looked around.

"Where's Kitten?" he said.

5.

She'd seen the toad sitting on a rock and picked it up as Zac was collapsing on the floor. It did not pee on her. She thought he might need it so she slipped it inside and gently closed the screen and then she turned away.

The dirt and grass felt cool and soft beneath her torn-up feet. She stopped after a few steps to dig a chunk of glass out of her heel. She flicked it into the dark and kept going, towards the Gulf. She undid the zipper at the back of her tartan skirt and let if fall as she walked. She looked up. There was half a moon dropping silver light upon the water and there were stars overhead. She thought she recognized Orion's belt but that was it for constellations, except for the little dipper or it might have been the big. She looked for Venus but didn't know which way it might be. She pulled off her top and left it behind her as she came to a short wall. A salt breeze moved off the bay. It was only in this hour, in these last lingering fingers of darkness that the air felt cool and clean.

Over the wall, just a drop of a few feet, there was a brief beach and then tiny waves lapping at the sand. She slid the knife out of her glove and placed it on top of the wall. She peeled off first one glove and then the other and left these on the wall as well then climbed over it, landing softly in the sand. She picked up the knife, undid the clasp, opened it and held it up to the moonlight. The blade sparkled and shined, the moonlight washed over it silver and blue. A flash of red from the oil rigs danced on the blade like firelight.

She saw a pier not far away, extending out beyond the waves. She took sliding sand steps towards it and as she walked she let the knife blade slide against her thigh, making delicate cuts from which tiny ribbons of red seeped.

She stepped onto the wooden boards and moved out over the black water, over the Gulf, she thought, over the void. As she walked, lights blinked far out to sea, as a glow grew at the eastern edge of the sea, and the stars turned overhead. The moon, with its crooked smile, looked down on her and she continued to slide the blade along her thigh. She dragged a bloody trail behind her before she came to the end of the pier and stopped.

She felt the hunk of metal in her mouth as it clinked against her teeth. It felt heavy and tasted bitter. She could feel the metal in her lips and ears, her nose and nipples, her clit and labia. She felt weighted down. She felt that if she stepped into the water she would sink right down to the bottom when what she really wanted to do was float up to the sky.

She set the knife on a pylon. With sticky hands she reached into her mouth, unscrewed the barbell and spat the pieces into the water. She undid the loops at the corners of her lips and flung them out into the dark. She sat, cross-legged and began to work on her ears. Each one came out with a pop or a snap or a rip, and she sent each one into the night, the deep.

She cracked apart the two in her nipples and tossed them away, and then she reached down and removed the one in her belly button, the first one she'd gotten. She kissed it and tossed it into the sea. She reached further down for the four hoops below and then, finally, at the last, the one in her clit. She removed this, placed it in her mouth with tin tasting fingers and swallowed it. She stood.

She felt naked now.

She felt her flesh and skin and felt for anything she might have missed. She felt the holes in her, the scars and burns. She reached inside herself just to make sure nothing had gotten lost in there.

She picked up the knife and sliced it across the sky.

"Kitten," a voice said.

She turned.

They stood before her. She held the blade in her hand.

They stood before her and she was naked and small. The sun was not yet climbing, the covers of the night not quite pulled back. The air of the sea smelled of salt and distant storms. It would soon collapse and drip with heat.

Raven, Sean and Zac watched as the hand holding the blade moved; watched its razor edge trace the curve of her breast colored in night shaded pinks, purple and blues. She drew the knife point in ripples across her skin, not pressing hard enough to cut, but stirring vibrations in the air, and then she pressed harder and blood seeped out.

"Kitten, don't," Raven said.

"Nothing does it anymore," Kitten said so quietly they could hardly hear. "No cutting, no burning, no slicing, no fucking. Nothing does it anymore."

"Kitten," Sean said. "We were just talking about our best part of the day." He moved towards her one step and then two. She backed away as far as the pier would allow. "We were just talking about how for all of us it was playing our gig, you know?" he said. "We're going to go on tour. We'll fuck the world."

"We need you," Raven said.

Kitten shook her head. "Nothing does it anymore." She pounded her fist against the side of her head. "No songs. No poems. No music. No art. No cunts or cocks or fucking apologies written on a grocery store-bought birthday card." She shook and trembled and set the tip of the blade to her chest.

"That could be a new song," Sean said.

"Sean!" Raven said.

"It's got a beat."

Raven turned back to Kitten whose eyes were wide and teeth were clenched. Her hands were wrapped around the handle of the knife. She placed it to her chest, set to plunge it into her beating heart.

"I don't want to live like this anymore," she said. "I don't."

Raven inched forward. "None of us do," Raven said. "But we do."

Kitten shook. The point of the knife began to part her skin.

"I can't," she said.

The muscles of her arms tensed, the scars rippled, the burns bubbled, and the veins in her hands popped. She would do it now, she would do it now this time for real and then a great shadow overtook her. She was lifted up towards the sky and released into the empty air. The knife flew from her hand as her mouth opened wide to gasp for a final breath. She saw the stars and the first rays of sun flashing across the Texas sky just before she hit the water.

6.

"What the fuck?" Raven screamed.

Sean couldn't say anything. He'd just seen Zac toss Kitten into the ocean and he couldn't believe it. They were two hundred feet from the shore.

"She can't swim!" Raven said.

"Stand up," Zac called out.

The black water below them churned and thrashed. An arm flung out and then a leg. There was a gasp for air and then a foot rose pale and white.

"Stand up!" Zac called out again.

Sean jumped into the water. It wrapped him up like warm velvet. He felt something smooth and shifting beneath his feet and was sure he'd just stepped on a shark. His head broke the surface and he gasped for air. He saw Kitten's face turning in horror to the stars and then it was gone, falling to the depths. He reached for her but her flailing limbs kept getting in the way.

"Oh, for fuck's sake," Zac said.

Zac jumped in near the thrashing bodies and stood. The rippling water barely covered his waist. He reached out and took hold of two small arms and heaved them up. "Stand up," he said.

Kitten blinked and gasped. Sean reached his feet to the deep. He felt sand. He stood. She did too. She saw Zac, his hair slicked down around his head. She put her weight into her legs and found that she could stand. The water was warm and held her. She looked up at the pier. By the growing glowing morning light, she saw Raven just a few feet up above her.

"Motherfucker," Sean said.

Kitten looked back at Zac.

"I can stand up," she said.

"Sandbar. Go ten feet in or out and you'll be in way over your head."

"Motherfucker!" Sean said.

"You threw me in," she said.

"Yup," Zac said.

"You asshole," she said and punched him in the arm. He laughed and splashed her in the face. She spit salt water and tried to punch him again. She missed and fell but found her feet quickly, swiped back her hair and looked around for something to punch again.

"Well, fuck --- if it's going to be a party," Sean said and hit the water with his arm, sending a great splash at the two of them. Kitten squealed. Zac laughed.

Raven saw them dancing in the sea; the boy too big for the world, the cut-up kitten-cat, and the fucked-up half-breed. She was the raven and the scarecrow, the goddess and the girl. Dawn was coming and she was afraid all those dreams of being a vampire might suddenly come true and the burst of light would turn her to ash.

"Do I have to come up there and toss you in too?" Zac said.

Raven shook her head. She bit her lip but couldn't stop a smile. Dawn came, the sun breached the east and she did not die. She saw a sailboat passing in the not-too-distant-distance.

She bent and unzipped her boots as Sean began to hoot.

"Take it off!" Kitten shouted.

Raven stepped out of the boots and craned her arms around to unzip her stained white dress. She let it slink down and fall and then pulled down her underwear. Zac, Sean and Kitten stood in the rippling golden waves. They watched as Raven lifted her face to the sky, reached out her arms and stood with nothing between her and the molten sun but her skin.

The End

29968220R00147

Made in the USA
Charleston, SC
31 May 2014